THE SILVERTON SCANDAL

Amanda Grange

CHIVERS
THORNDIKE

This Large Print edition is published by BBC Audiobooks Ltd, Bath, England and by Thorndike Press, Waterville, Maine, USA.

Published in 2004 in the U.K. by arrangement with Robert Hale Ltd.

Published in 2004 in the U.S. by arrangement with Robert Hale Limited.

U.K. Hardcover   ISBN 0–7540–5692–9 (Chivers Large Print)
U.K. Softcover   ISBN 0–7540–7683–0 (Camden Large Print)
U.S. Softcover   ISBN 0–7862–5955–8 (General)

The text of this Large Print edition is unabridged.
Other aspects of the book may vary from the original edition.

Set in 16 pt. New Times Roman.

Printed in Great Britain on acid-free paper.

British Library Cataloguing in Publication Data available

Library of Congress Cataloging-in-Publication Data

Grange, Amanda.
    The Silverton scandal / Amanda Grange.
        p.   cm.
    ISBN 0–7862–5955–8 (lg. print : sc : alk. paper)
    1. Brigands and robbers—Fiction. 2. Nobility—Fiction.
    3. England—Fiction. 4. Large type books. I. Title.
PR6107.R35S55 2004
823'.92—dc22   2003060139

CHAPTER ONE

'Well, miss, what's it to be?' asked the coachman. 'Are you coming or aren't you?'

Miss Eleanor Grantham, standing in the yard of the coaching inn, hesitated. She had not been intending to leave Bath. In fact, nothing could have been further from her thoughts when she had left the house that morning. But events had taken an unexpected turn, and she was tempted to board the stage.

She glanced across the yard to where Mr Kendrick, a middle-aged and apparently respectable gentleman, was saying goodbye to his companion, a stocky man with dark-brown hair. She hesitated for one moment longer, and then took her decision.

'Yes,' she said.

Her ticket purchased, she followed Mr Kendrick on to the coach. Several more passengers followed, the door was shut and the coach pulled away. As it rolled out of the inn yard, to a chorus of ostlers shouting, horns blowing, dogs barking and horses neighing, Eleanor looked determinedly out of the window. She did not want to look at Mr Kendrick, in case her revulsion showed.

It was difficult to believe that he was a blackmailer, she thought, as she caught sight of his reflection in the windowpane. In his

1

well-cut tail-coat, with his white linen and neatly arranged cravat, he looked like a prosperous businessman. But she was in no doubt about his identity. He was exactly as Arabella had described him. As she thought of her younger sister, Eleanor's face softened. Arabella was adorable, and was soon going to be married. If, that was, Mr Kendrick did not ruin it by sending the letters to Arabella's fiancé.

Mr Kendrick was sitting directly opposite her, with a case held tightly across his knees. What was in it? wondered Eleanor. Could it possibly be her sister's letters?

It was strange to think that they could be the source of so much worry. Written some five years earlier, in the autumn of 1805, they contained the childish effusions of a young Arabella who had at the time been still in the schoolroom. Arabella had written them to her best friend's brother, a flamboyant young man who fancied himself a poet. He had dedicated his *Ode to an Angel's Hair* and his *Sonnet to a Fairy's Eyes* to Arabella, and this had appealed to her schoolgirl fancy. In return she had written him several grateful letters, which, following a burglary, had unluckily fallen into the hands of Mr Kendrick. And now, if Arabella did not meet Mr Kendrick's demands, he had threatened to send the letters to Charles.

A thousand guineas! thought Eleanor, as

2

she recalled Mr Kendrick's price. It was a ridiculous sum.

Arabella had told Mr Kendrick she did not have such a large amount of money, but he had only laughed at her. He had told her that she looked like a clever girl, and had said that as she was shortly to marry the heir to a dukedom, she would know how to get it.

Eleanor shook her head at Mr Kendrick's mistake. Arabella was not a clever girl. In fact, she was as artless as the day was long. She would never even have thought of trying to inveigle the money out of Charles, and instead she had confided in Eleanor. And Eleanor, as always protecting her younger sister, had promised to see Mr Kendrick herself.

She fixed her attention on the passing scenery. The autumn countryside was glowing with reds, oranges and yellows, as the leaves on the trees changed colour and fluttered to the ground. But the sight, lovely though it was, could not distract her thoughts for long.

She had visited Mr Kendrick's house that morning, but her visit had proved fruitless. He had left the house, his housekeeper had informed Eleanor, and was on his way to London. And so it was that Eleanor had followed him to the coaching inn and finally boarded the stage.

The coach rolled on.

Eleanor turned her attention back to the countryside, and by and by she found herself soothed by the sight. The fields were a rich green, and were glowing beneath the autumn sun. The verges were full of wild flowers, and the trees, with their ever-changing colours, were bright and cheerful. Villages, towns and cities passed by.

At length, the afternoon gave way to early evening, and the light began to fail.

'Not much further now,' said the clergyman sitting next to Eleanor. 'Then we'll be stopping for the night.'

Eleanor was relieved. Though not uncomfortable, the journey had been long and she was looking forward to a rest. Even so, she was apprehensive about what would happen when the coach stopped. She must speak to Mr Kendrick, that much was clear, but she had no idea whether he could be made to return the letters for the fifty guineas she had in her purse. She hoped so. But if he couldn't, what then?

Fortunately, at that moment, her despondent thoughts were broken into by the sound of galloping hoofs. She looked out of the window. The stagecoach had met with few other travellers on its journey, and none at all since dusk had started to fall. The horseman provided her thoughts with a welcome distraction. She was just wondering whether it would be a young buck, riding to a local dinner party, or a man of commerce, returning home after a busy day, when a loud cry rent the air.

4

'Stand and deliver!'

There was a moment of disbelief as the passengers looked at one another, and then a mood of panic broke out in the coach. The bony clergyman crossed himself, crying, 'Lord, spare us!' whilst the stout matron sitting next to him gasped, 'Mercy me!'

Mr Kendrick did not seem frightened. He did, however, hold on to his case more tightly than ever.

What a pity, thought Eleanor. If he had let go of it, then in the confusion she might have been able to open it and see if the letters were inside. As he was leaving Bath, there was a possibility that he had decided to take Arabella's letters with him. They were worth a great deal of money to him if he could blackmail Arabella into paying him 1000 guineas for them, and he would probably not want to leave anything so valuable behind. But there was no chance of her looking now.

She glanced out of the window to see what was happening. The coach driver was wrestling with the horses and trying to stop them rearing as he brought the coach to a sudden halt. Ahead of him, sitting astride a coal-black horse, was a tall figure swathed in a dark cloak. Eleanor peered through the gloom and tried to make out the highwayman's features, but even in the daylight it would have been difficult, and in the fading light it was impossible. A black handkerchief was tied

5

across the lower half of his face, and a tricorne hat was pulled down low over his eyes.

Motioning with his pistols the highwayman ordered the coachman down from his box. Then he turned his attention to the passengers on the roof and indicated that they were to follow. When they were lined up in a row at the side of the road, the highwayman rode over to the door of the coach. His eyes ran over the passengers inside and one by one they looked away, unable to meet his gaze. But Eleanor did not. Instead of looking away she returned his regard.

So this is what a highwayman is like, she thought.

He was tall, and dark, and controlled his dancing horse with ease. His face was largely hidden, but because she was looking up at him Eleanor found that she could see his eyes, which would otherwise have been concealed by the shadow of his hat. They were steely blue. And they were looking directly into her own. They traced the lines of her face, dropping from her hazel eyes to her fine cheekbones and full mouth, and unaccountably she shivered. At first she thought she must be afraid. But no, the shiver did not feel like fear. It was more like . . . she shook her head. She could not place it. Still, whatever it was, she was determined not to let it show. She lifted her chin a fraction. Just for a moment she thought she saw a glimmer of respect in the

6

highwayman's eyes, but she must be mistaken. No highwayman would feel respect for one of his victims. A moment later the expression was gone, and she was left with the belief that she must have imagined it, for nothing now remained in his eyes but the cold ruthlessness she would have expected.

Breaking their locked gaze he danced his horse back a few paces and gestured for the passengers to disembark.

There was a commotion inside the coach. The stout matron pulled her shawl more firmly around her shoulders. She gripped the handle of her basket extra tightly before pushing open the door and climbing out, spilling an apple out of her basket in the process.

The clergyman crossed himself before exclaiming, 'May the good Lord protect us!' and following her down the steps.

Mr Kendrick motioned Eleanor to go next. He still had tight hold of his case, and again she wondered what was inside. But now was not the time for wondering. She bent to retrieve the matron's apple before stepping out of the coach.

The night air was cold, and she was glad of her cloak. The wind stung her cheeks and whipped at the tendrils of dark-brown hair which had escaped from her chignon. It tugged at the pins that held it up, threatening to spill her hair about her shoulders. She reached up and pushed them securely into place.

'Here,' she said to the matron, dropping the apple back into the basket, 'you lost this.'

'Oh, thank you, my dear,' said the matron. 'Though a lost apple's the least of our worries.' She glanced at the highwayman, who watched impassively as the last passenger, Mr Kendrick, climbed out of the coach.

Once all the passengers were clear of the coach, he said tersely, 'Over there.'

Controlling his dancing horse with light hands he motioned them to join the other passengers and the coachmen, who were standing at the side of the road.

'Now. Your valuables,' he said. He dismounted in one lithe movement. 'You there,' he called to the stout matron. 'Empty your basket.'

The matron, flustered, started to do as he said, but she was so nervous that she dropped it.

He took a step towards her, but Eleanor was too quick for him. Stepping protectively in front of the quivering matron she said, 'Leave her alone.'

She spoke boldly, but as soon as she had started to speak a part of her was already beginning to regret it. The highwayman was large and dark. Now that she was standing in front of him she could tell that he was over six feet tall. His cloak accentuated his broad shoulders. Beneath it he was dressed all in black. A black coat was pulled across his chest and tight black breeches were stretched over his muscular thighs. He was strong and commanding. And dangerous.

He stopped dead and fixed his eyes on her. Her heart began to pound. Nevertheless she held her ground.

She was still looking up at him, but the angle was not as sharp as it had been when she had been sitting in the coach, and she could no longer see his eyes. They were hidden in the shadow of his hat. Still, she could imagine them burning with a cold blue flame. She felt her legs begin to shake.

'Can't you see she's frightened?' Eleanor demanded, knowing she must speak before her courage deserted her.

His eyes narrowed. 'Whereas you, it would seem, are not.'

She looked at him defiantly, whilst all the time knowing that he could not be more wrong, but she was determined not to show it. 'I have never been afraid of bullies,' she declared.

As soon as she had spoken she knew she had hit a nerve. His whole body tensed. She could see it in the lift of his shoulders and the firming of the muscles beneath his coat. And she could see it in the tightening of his hands—large, strong hands—around the handles of his pistols.

She held her breath.

'Bullies?' Beneath his mask she saw his jaw

clamp, and there was a perilous edge to his voice.

She should say no more. She had taken enough chances. But though her palms were damp and her heart was thudding in her chest, something drove her on.

'Yes. Bullies. Or perhaps you think that holding up a coach full of clergymen, women and young boys is a sign of bravery?' she enquired bitingly.

And now she knew what it was that drove her. It was more than just her anger at being held up at gunpoint, it was her anger towards those who would threaten the safety and happiness of perfectly innocent people. Mr Kendrick had threatened her sister's safety, not by holding her at gunpoint, but by threatening her happiness with a handful of childish letters written when she was still in the schoolroom, and now here was this man threatening a group of similarly innocent and inoffensive people. And she had to give vent to her anger, no matter how rash it might be.

She could feel the tension in him, and she could feel her fellow passengers' amazement. All conversation, muted and rebellious though it had been, ceased. The night was suddenly silent.

'Sometimes . . .'

The highwayman's voice was so soft and husky that she could barely hear him.

'. . . such actions are necessary.'

She wondered whether she could have heard him properly. His remark was so unexpected that she was momentarily disconcerted. She had expected him to brag about his exploit, or perhaps laugh mockingly and push her aside, but instead his reply had been enigmatic. There was something unfathomable about his words. It was as though they contained a hidden meaning, but what could it be?

A moment later she took control of herself. That was nonsense. She was letting his magnetism cloud her judgement. For there was no denying the fact that he was magnetic. Something about him, something beyond his tall lithe body and steely blue eyes, compelled her attention.

Was it his stance? she wondered. It was strong and powerful, like the man himself. Or was it the force she felt emanating from him? Or was it something more nebulous, and yet real for all that? A mixture of mystery and intrigue that enveloped him as surely as his cloak?

Angrily she shook away her unsettling thoughts. Despite his magnetism, he was a common highwayman, and she had better not forget it.

'I'm glad you're not afraid,' he said at last. His shoulders relaxed, and his voice lost some of its tension. 'I need someone to help me, and you've just elected yourself. Empty the basket

11

and follow me.' Without waiting for an answer he turned his attention to the other travellers. 'You will drop your valuables in the basket as I walk down the line, and then take three steps back. Do you understand?'

There was a murmur of rebellion from the young men, but although several of them bunched their fists, and one even took half a step forwards, they wilted beneath his gaze. One by one they muttered a reluctant agreement.

'Good.' His tone relented slightly. 'Do as I say and you will have nothing to fear.'

The fact that his attention was momentarily on her fellow travellers did not escape Eleanor's notice. With a further spurt of rashness she asked herself whether she would be able to disarm him. She had no intention of helping him to rob her fellow travellers if she could avoid it, but reluctantly she realized that disarming him was out of the question. Even if she managed to knock one of the pistols from his hand he would still have the other one, and he would be prepared to use it. But if she went along with him for the time being, then a better opportunity to foil him might present itself.

She bent down and picked up the matron's basket. Carefully setting the contents—a couple of jars of home-made jam, a shawl, a large bag of apples and a cushion—on to the ground she reluctantly followed the highwayman.

The highwayman, meantime, had walked up to the first of the passengers, a young gentleman who had been sitting on the roof.

'Hand over your valuables,' he commanded.

The young man snarled but he emptied his pockets nevertheless, dropping a collection of sovereigns into Eleanor's basket with a *chink*.

'And the rest,' remarked the highwayman.

The young man glowered, but he pulled off his gold signet ring and dropped it on top of the sovereigns, then followed it with his fob watch.

One by one the passengers emptied their pockets and purses, dropping first money and then watches, bracelets and necklaces into the basket. The young men on the roof were followed by the clergyman and then the matron, leaving Mr Kendrick until last.

Eleanor tensed as the highwayman drew level with him. Would Mr Kendrick open his case?

She felt her pulse begin to quicken. If she was lucky, the unexpected hold-up might offer her a chance of rescuing Arabella's letters without having to speak to Mr Kendrick at all. If the letters were in the case she might find an opportunity to seize them when Mr Kendrick's attention was elsewhere, for she felt sure the highwayman would have no interest in them.

As Mr Kendrick began to empty his pockets she held her breath. He handed over a considerable amount of money, together with his watch and a gold ring, dropping them into her by now almost full basket, but he did not open the case.

Would the highwayman care? He had what he wanted. Perhaps he would not trouble himself over it. Eleanor glanced towards him. To see that his gaze had dropped to the slim leather case.

'What's inside?'

'Nothing of any interest.' Mr Kendrick spoke smoothly, but there was something wary about him.

'Open it.'

The highwayman's command was curt.

Mr Kendrick made no move to do so, which surprised Eleanor. As a blackmailer, she had assumed he would be a coward, but there was a look of determination on his face that made her reconsider and she wondered how the encounter would progress.

She looked from Mr Kendrick to the highwayman, who was just as determined.

She looked back to Mr Kendrick and saw Mr Kendrick's expression alter slightly.

He is going to try and reason with him, she thought.

'The case contains nothing of value,' said Mr Kendrick evenly. 'Just some business documents. They would be of no interest to you.'

The temperature dropped by several

degrees. An icy wind sprang up and whipped at the hem of the highwayman's cloak, blowing it out around him and making him look even larger than before.

'Open it,' he said again.

When Mr Kendrick did not comply, the highwayman slipped one pistol into the top of his breeches and with his free hand grasped the case, but still Mr Kendrick held it tight.

There was a tense moment as the two men's eyes met.

'Nothing of value, eh?' said the highwayman. He gave it a tug. 'Then you won't mind parting with it.'

'The documents are of value to me,' said Mr Kendrick desperately. 'I don't want to lose them. They would be very difficult to replace. But they would be worth nothing to anyone else.'

The highwayman's eyes hardened. 'I'll be the judge of that.' He wrenched the case out of Mr Kendrick's grip. Still holding the case, the highwayman glanced at the basket, which glittered and glimmered with gold and diamonds. 'A worthy haul. And now, ladies and gentlemen, I thank you for your co-operation, and I will be on my way.'

He turned to Eleanor, and she held out the basket to him. He was holding the case in one hand, however, and a pistol in the other, so that instead of taking it he said, 'You will carry it for me.'

15

He inclined his head in the direction of his horse, a magnificent black stallion that stood snorting nearby.

Eleanor hesitated. It was not a peaceable-looking animal, and she was afraid to go too close.

'Don't worry, he won't hurt you,' came the highwayman's soft voice. Then, sardonically, he said, 'He is not as dangerous as I am.'

The mocking tone in his voice stiffened Eleanor's spine and gave her all the courage she needed. Squaring her shoulders, she went over to the horse.

The highwayman followed her, walking backwards and keeping the pistol levelled at the other passengers to hold them at bay.

'Now, take the contents of the basket and put them into my saddle-bags,' he said. 'Split the contents evenly between the two and fasten them when you have done.'

He spoke in an aside. His attention was still on the coachmen and travellers, who were beginning to look mutinous.

Eleanor cast a covert glance towards the pistol that was tucked into the top of his breeches. If she made a grab for it then he, with a pistol in one hand and the case in the other, would not be able to stop her. He might, it was true, level his own pistol at her, but if her hand was on the other one . . . Tucked into his breeches as it was, she felt sure he would not take the chance of her pulling the trigger.

She summoned her courage and, without giving herself time to think about it, she passed the basket into her left hand and reached for his pistol with her right.

Quicker than thought he dropped the case and before she knew what was happening his fingers had closed tightly over her own. Her hand might be on the pistol . . . but his hand was on hers.

'I wouldn't do that if I were you.'

His voice was level but it held an edge of steel.

Eleanor swallowed. She wished she could threaten to shoot, but he had been too quick for her, and although her hand rested on the handle, her finger was nowhere near the trigger. Loath though she was to admit it, she was beaten.

'It was a good try,' he said, his fingers still closed about her own. 'But let me give you a word of warning. If you ever find yourself faced with a highwayman again, don't attempt such a rash action. Another highwayman might not be as . . . forgiving . . . as I am.'

Then his strong hand closed more firmly around her fingers and he prised them loose.

Eleanor instinctively glanced down. His hand was large. The long fingers tapered towards the end. Her own hand, enclosed within it, looked tiny. The sight made her feel vulnerable. She tried to draw her hand back, but instead of letting it go he held on to it. He

17

ought by rights to have relinquished it. Once he had prised her fingers loose of the pistol he should have let them go. But instead he held them in his own. Through her glove, and through his glove, she was aware of the touch of his fingers. It was firm and hard . . . and it burned.

Her eyes widened, and without her volition they rose to his own. Their gazes met. She was so close to him that the brim of his hat no longer shaded his eyes, and she saw that beneath their steeliness they were as blue as a summer sky. Dark brows arched over them, and a lock of black hair fell across his forehead.

His fingers once again locked around her own, but this time there was a gentleness that had not been there before, and in a surprisingly courtly gesture he lifted her hand.

She froze, held motionless by some strange force that robbed her of control of her body, and without realizing what she was doing she held her breath. It was only for a moment, but a moment was all he needed. Bending his head, he brushed his mouth over the back of her hand. She gasped as a sudden crackle of energy ran over her skin. It caused her eyes to widen as they were held by his. She saw his steely eyes smoulder, and knew by the sudden fire that he had felt the potent force as well.

And then she began to regain her senses. The incident had been strange and disturbing.

If she had experienced such a strong reaction when any other man had kissed her hand she would have found it exhilarating, but to have it happen with a highwayman . . . it was mortifying.

In confusion, she tried to reclaim her hand. For a moment he held on to it, but then he allowed it to slide through his fingers. Even so, his eyes continued to gaze into hers. Then, with a last steely glance, he grasped the basket and emptied the contents into his saddle-bag before casting it aside.

Eleanor stepped back.

'As for *your* purse . . .' he said.

She lifted her chin. Her purse contained fifty guineas, the remnants of a legacy, and it was all she and Arabella possessed. She must hold on to it if she was to have a chance of buying back Arabella's letters.

But instead of demanding it, his eyes danced. 'You can keep it,' he said.

With one last burning glance he mounted his horse and rode away. She watched him go. Despite her horror at what he had done, she could not tear her eyes away from him.

Once he had disappeared from view, she became aware that a hubbub had broken out amongst the passengers. One of the young men from the roof was demanding that the coachman should follow the highwayman.

'With what?' snorted the coachman, hands on hips.

The other passengers were beginning to take sides, some unreasonably demanding that the coachman follow the highwayman, whilst others were demanding to be taken on their way.

'Unharness a horse!' said the young man, already running towards one.

'It is too late for that, my son,' said the clergyman, putting a hand on his arm. 'Never fear, the good lord will make sure he doesn't escape his punishment.'

'Pah!' The young man shook off the clergyman.

'You'll never catch him on one of those, Mark,' said another young gentleman. 'Didn't you see what he was riding? The devil certainly knows his horseflesh. He'll be miles away before you can get one of the carriage horses out of the traces.'

'Damn!' said the young man, letting go of the harness in frustration. 'The one time I win at cards, and that—'

The clergyman coughed meaningfully.

'That *rascal*,' said the young man, glancing towards the ladies and swallowing down the more forthright word he had been about to use, 'has to take every sovereign.'

Eleanor was by now standing next to Mr Kendrick.

'I hope you didn't lose anything too important,' she said, hoping against hope that he might be unsettled enough to tell her what had been in the case, for if he let slip that the letters had been there then Arabella was safe.

But she was not to be so fortunate. Mr Kendrick did not look perturbed. 'No,' he replied noncommitally.

'It must be worse to lose papers than money,' she ventured, determined to make the most of the opportunity that had presented itself. 'I know how hard letters are to replace.'

Unfortunately, Mr Kendrick did not rise to her bait. Eleanor gave an inward sigh. She had hoped to startle him into some kind of admission but she was no further forward than she had been an hour ago. There was only one thing for it. She would have to broach the subject directly. Seizing the moment she opened her mouth, but before she could speak, Mr Kendrick excused himself and went over to the coachman, lending him a hand in calming the horses, which had become skittish during the incident.

Eleanor swallowed a cry of vexation. She would have to wait until the coach reached London and speak to Mr Kendrick then. Her spirits sank. She was not looking forward to it. Still, it must be done. It was the reason for her journey, after all. And at least she still had her purse. As soon as the horses were calmed, the coachman became businesslike once again.

'All aboard,' he called, climbing on to the box. 'We've lost enough time as it is.'

The passengers responded quickly, boarding

21

the coach with a minimum of fuss and settling themselves once more in their seats. Eleanor had just taken her place when the coach gave a lurch and then it pulled away.

'I want to thank you, my dear,' said the stout matron as they set off again. 'If you hadn't come to my rescue I don't know what I would have done.'

'These are lawless times we live in,' said the clergyman, shaking his head. 'It's all the fault of Napoleon. He's taken our best men away from us. They're all fighting on the Continent.'

The matron nodded. 'Sam, my youngest— and never a better boy drew breath—has gone for a soldier. Fighting for king and country, he is.'

'And my nephew,' remarked the clergyman.

The hold-up provided a fruitful source of gossip, with much exclaiming on the state of the country, the iniquities of the criminal classes, and the bravery of the fine young men who had joined the army in order to stop the Corsican monster in his tracks.

The coach continued on its way across the countryside, eventually pulling into the yard of a respectable coaching inn. It was a long, low half-timbered building. A number of passengers climbed out. To Eleanor's surprise, one of them was Mr Kendrick. His housekeeper had declared that he was going to London, but either the woman had been mistaken, or he was going to break his journey. Eleanor's spirits rose. It seemed her luck had changed. She knew the inn, and the neighbourhood, for Mrs Lydia Fairacres, one of her mother's seminary friends, lived there. And since her mother's death, Lydia and her husband Frederick had been good friends to Eleanor and Arabella. Indeed, Frederick was to give Arabella away at her wedding.

As Eleanor climbed out of the coach she kept a close eye on Mr Kendrick to see where he went. Twilight had fallen, but lanterns had been lit to counteract the gathering gloom, and she saw him weave his way in and out of the postboys, past a carriage whose horses were being changed and on in the direction of the road.

She slipped through a crowd of travellers, past a well-dressed lady who was emerging from her carriage, a postboy, and a footman unloading a private coach. Then she discreetly followed him . . . only to see a private carriage roll up beside him as he reached the road. He glanced quickly to left and right, climbed into the carriage and it pulled away.

'No!' exclaimed Eleanor out loud.

She felt a wave of frustration wash over her. After all she had been through, to lose him at the last moment was too vexing. And not only was it vexing, but it left her with a very real problem, namely, how was she to find him again?

She let out a long sigh. She had come so far,

and yet she had been defeated at the last.

Still, things would look better in the morning, she consoled herself. Abandoning her quest for the present, Eleanor went into the inn to enquire about a carriage to take her to Lydia's home, Fairacres Park.

No sooner had she set foot over the threshold, however, when she was accosted from behind—and turned round to see Lydia herself.

Lydia was looking as elegant as usual. Her lilac pelisse was in the first stare of fashion, and her bonnet, with its curled ostrich-feather, was a dream.

'My dear Eleanor!' exclaimed Lydia. 'I thought it was you! What are you doing here? And why didn't you tell me you were coming? What a wonderful surprise.'

'Lydia!' Overcoming her astonishment, Eleanor greeted the older woman warmly, and returned her embrace. 'I would have let you know I was coming if I could, but my journey was arranged at such short notice that—'

Lydia nodded sagely. 'My dear, there's no need to explain. I know just what it's like when you are organizing a wedding. The duchess might be seeing to most of the arrangements, but there must still be a hundred and one things for you to do. And so you are on your way to London to try on your dress, I suppose.'

Eleanor was about to contradict her, but then changed her mind. If Lydia had assumed

24

she was travelling to London in order to have a fitting for a new gown to wear at Arabella's wedding then so be it: she did not feel equal to the task of explaining the real situation just at the moment, and in such a public place.

'I don't blame you,' Lydia went on. 'You must have something stylish to wear for the occasion. And who knows,' she added innocently, 'with so many eligible young gentlemen attending, you might meet a husband of your own.'

Eleanor suppressed a smile. Lydia's matchmaking instincts would not allow her to accept that Eleanor was now six-and-twenty, and as such on the shelf, and she insisted on making hopeful comments every time they met.

'For you know, a society wedding is just the sort of place to meet a husband,' continued Lydia. 'There will be any number of dukes, earls and barons, all thinking about marriage. What better place to find your destiny?'

'I don't think dukes, earls and barons will want to marry a penniless young lady with no connections,' Eleanor pointed out with a smile.

'Why not?' Lydia challenged her. 'Charles did.'

The point was unarguable. Charles had been happy to propose to the penniless Arabella. But then, Arabella had qualities to counteract her lack of fortune and connections. Golden hair and cornflower-blue eyes, a sweet nature and a delectably tiny figure, were all powerful inducements to ignore her other shortcomings. Whereas Eleanor's brown hair and plain features were not.

Eleanor, however, did not point this out, for Lydia would have immediately recommended a variety of lotions for brightening her hair and improving her complexion, and would not have rested until she had tried them all!

'But we can't stand here gossiping all day. We have to get back home. It is lucky I bumped into you,' Lydia said, taking Eleanor's arm. 'You don't want to spend the night in an inn. You must stay with us. It will be far more comfortable, I promise you.'

Eleanor gave her heartfelt thanks for the invitation and readily agreed.

'I am looking forward to the wedding,' said Lydia as the two ladies went over to Lydia's smart carriage. 'And Frederick is very pleased to be giving Arabella away. He—but I must let you fetch your bag,' said Lydia, suddenly noticing that Eleanor did not have a valise. 'I suppose it is at the inn.'

Eleanor was just about to say that she did not have a valise, when Lydia forestalled her. 'Unless you were on the stagecoach, the one that was held up by the highwayman? The news is all round the inn.'

'Already?' asked Eleanor in surprise.

'Bad news always travels quickly,' said

26

Lydia. 'As soon as the first passenger walked through the door and declared he needed a double brandy, for he had just been held up by a highwayman, the inn was buzzing with the news.'

Eleanor gave a wry smile. It would be the young gentleman who had complained so bitterly about having his winnings stolen, she imagined. But Lydia was right. Bad news did travel quickly.

'Yes, I was,' she acknowledged.

'Oh! How wonderful! That is, how terrible!' Lydia said, suddenly recollecting that she ought not to exclaim quite so happily over Eleanor's misfortune. 'I do hope you have not been hurt?'

'No, not at all.'

'Oh, good.' Reassured that Eleanor was all right, Lydia was free to enjoy the sensational happening. 'It will be something exciting to talk about over dinner.' Then her face fell. 'Frederick will be incensed. He is the local magistrate,' she reminded Eleanor, 'and he will be annoyed that it has happened here, right under his nose.' She sighed. 'And it will fall to him to investigate the incident. Which means that we will not find him at home when we return. It is such a nuisance, for we have a house full of guests. And I have already had to leave them which, of course, as the hostess, I did not want to do. But I have had a raging toothache and I could bear it no longer. I had to come into town to have it attended to.'

'It doesn't need to come out, I hope?' asked Eleanor sympathetically, glad to forget about her own troubles for a while.

'Fortunately not. Apparently the tooth is sound and the problem should clear up of its own accord. I can't tell you what a relief it is!'

They reached the carriage, with its highly polished brasswork, and comfortable pink-upholstered squabs. A liveried footman let down the step and handed them in, and then folded up the step and shut the door behind them. And then they were on their way.

As Eleanor settled herself back against the squabs she remarked casually, 'Do you know a Mr Kendrick?'

The fact that he had been met by a private carriage at the coaching inn implied that he was staying in the area, and in that case it occurred to her that Lydia might know him. If fortune favoured her, she might be able to discover where he was and to learn something about him, so that she would have an idea of how to approach him over the matter of Arabella's letters.

Lydia became thoughtful. 'No, I don't think I do. Why?'

'Oh, no reason. It is just that he was on the coach, and he was then met by a private carriage, which led me to think he might be a neighbour of yours.'

Lydia shook her head. 'No. The name is not

familiar.'

Eleanor swallowed her disappointment but it was possible that Frederick might know something about him. Perhaps Frederick would even be able to give her some help and advice on how to deal with him. She had thought of consulting Frederick when Arabella had first confided in her, but in order to keep Arabella's confidence she had decided to try and solve the problem on her own before involving anyone else.

It was not far to Fairacres Park. In less than a quarter of an hour the carriage turned off the road and bowled along a broad drive before coming to a halt. The building was an elegant one. Its golden stone glowed in the lamplight and its elegant proportions gave it a peaceful, tranquil air. The façade was lined by tall windows, and from them came a welcoming stream of light.

As the carriage finally rolled to a halt, Eleanor and Lydia were handed out by a footman, and together they entered the house.

Eleanor looked round the familiar hall with pleasure. She had visited the house on a number of occasions, and it held many happy memories. The hallway was impressive. Large marble pillars rose gracefully to the high ceiling, where they were ornamented round the top with gold acanthus leaves. Beyond them, a splendid staircase curved upwards to the first floor. Family portraits were arranged neatly on the pale walls, and there was a black-and-white floor.

Lydia divested herself of her outdoor things, revealing her expertly arranged hair and trim figure. Eleanor, too, slipped off her cloak and pelisse, and became suddenly conscious of the fact that her brown muslin dress was three years old. Although the style was not dated—its high waist and puffed sleeves were as much in vogue as they had ever been—it had a patch near the bottom where she had torn it whilst digging in the garden.

Lydia, however, was too polite to notice, and having said how well Eleanor looked she turned to the butler and enquired, 'Where is everyone?'

'They are assembled in the drawing-room, madam,' he replied deferentially.

'Oh, good.' She turned to Eleanor. 'Then you will be able to meet them all before they retire to dress for dinner.' Turning to the butler again, she went on, 'Inform Mrs Hingis we have another guest and instruct her to make up the blue room, if you please, Tompkins.'

'Very good, madam,' he said, before withdrawing to make the necessary arrangements.

Eleanor followed Lydia into the drawing-room, where the other house guests were passing the time until it was time to dress for dinner. It was an elegant apartment, and although not quite as grand as the hall, it had a large marble fireplace and impressive white mouldings on the walls.

The room was full of guests. There was a young girl with her mother, an elegant woman just beyond the first flush of youth, two respectable-looking gentlemen, and over by the far wall, with his back towards her, a tall, lean gentleman with black hair.

'Everyone, we have a new guest in our midst,' said Lydia.

Eleanor turned her attention back to her hostess.

'Miss Grantham, one of my dearest friends' daughters, is here. She was on a stagecoach which has just been held up, and a monster of a highwayman took everything but her clothes,' she said. 'She is going to be staying with us, but you are not allowed to ask her anything about her ordeal until she has had something to eat.' She turned to Eleanor. 'And now, let me introduce you to everyone, Eleanor, my dear.'

As Lydia went through a list of names, Eleanor found her attention once again drawn to the gentleman standing in the corner. Continuing to pour his drink, he did not look round as she was introduced to the rest of the guests.

'This is Mrs Benson,' said Lydia, continuing with the introductions.

Eleanor murmured something politely as

she was introduced to the glamorous Mrs Benson.

'And that's just about everybody,' said Lydia. 'Except, of course, for Lord Silverton.'

At this, the tall man in the corner slowly turned. Eleanor saw a lean, tanned face, with olive skin drawn tightly across high cheekbones, a straight nose, a firm jaw and deeply cleft chin. Black hair framed his face ... and a pair of steely blue eyes met her own.

A feeling of foreboding washed over her. But he gave no sign of recognition, and she thought she must be mistaken.

'Lord Silverton, allow me to introduce Miss Grantham,' said Lydia.

Eleanor watched him as he crossed the room towards her. His hard muscles rippled beneath his black tail coat, and his stride was one of predatory grace.

'Miss Grantham,' he murmured, taking her hand.

He lifted it to his lips and kissed it. As he did so, a surge of energy ran up her arm and down her spine, leaving her tingling from head to foot.

Her eyes flew open.

Impossible! she thought.

But impossible or not, Lord Silverton was the highwayman.

CHAPTER TWO

And now what do I do? Eleanor thought, as Lydia continued to introduce her to the other guests. *Do I expose him for being a thief?*

She decided against it. She couldn't do that in front of everyone, it would be too embarrassing for Lydia. And besides, even if she did expose him, who would believe her? Lord Silverton was evidently a man of some standing. It was unlikely that anyone would accept her word for it if she said that he was the man who had held up the stagecoach.

And yet what was the alternative? To say nothing, and let him get away with his crime? At the thought of the clergyman's fear, and the stout matron's anguish, she nearly spoke. But again some instinct stopped her. For as well as thinking that no one would believe her, she found the situation odd. Lord Silverton was evidently a wealthy nobleman, and moreover he was a friend of Lydia and Frederick—and Frederick was a magistrate. Why, then, would he dress as a highwayman and hold up a stagecoach? It was perplexing.

Could she be mistaken? she wondered.

But no. She knew she was not.

Which left her pondering the question, why had he done it? A spirit of devilment? That explanation did not satisfy her. Lord Silverton was some thirty years of age, and was too old to indulge in such a prank. She had the instinctive feeling there was more to the situation—and to Lord Silverton—than met the eye.

'And that is everybody,' said Lydia, bringing Eleanor's thoughts back to the present.

Lord Silverton moved away, and Eleanor had to struggle to keep her eyes from following him. He drew her attention like a magnet, but she knew she must fight the impulse to watch him if she did not want to cause comment. Fortunately, her restraint was not tried too far, because at that moment the gong rang in the hall outside. It was time to dress for dinner.

'I'll show you to your room,' said Lydia, as the other guests made their way upstairs. 'It won't have been made up properly yet, but you will be able to refresh yourself before we eat. There isn't really time for you to change—will you mind dining as you are? I would be happy to lend you some clothes, but by the time I have found you anything suitable the dinner will be spoiled.'

Eleanor assured her that she had no objection to appearing for dinner in her plain muslin dress if her hostess did not mind.

Eleanor accompanied Lydia up the elegant sweeping staircase and along a maze of corridors before arriving at the bedroom.

'I'll send a maid along in a minute. If you

need anything, you have only to ask, and she will fetch it for you,' Lydia said.

Eleanor thanked her and, once she had left, closed the door. She gave a sigh of relief. Lydia was a kind hostess, but it was good to be on her own at last. She could still hardly believe everything that had happened to her in the last twenty-four hours: her sister's confidence, her visit to Mr Kendrick's Bath address, her spontaneous coach journey, the highwayman, the meeting with Lord Silverton . . . all had taken their toll. Thank goodness she had an opportunity to rest.

She looked around the bedroom with approval. Silk panels covered the walls, and a matching counterpane was spread over the half-tester bed. Facing the bed was a mahogany mantelpiece, intricately carved with bunches of grapes, and next to it was a washstand. Above the mantelpiece hung a gilded mirror, and on either side of it were wall sconces. The candles were lit, and a warm glow spread over the room.

Eleanor felt the tension of the day begin to ebb, and she sank gratefully on to the bed. It was soft, and she sank in to it with pleasure. It was just what she needed after spending all day in a coach, being forced to sit on an uncomfortable seat.

There was a scratching at the door and a minute later a neat little maid entered the room with a jug of hot water. She carried it over to the washstand and put it down carefully.

'Shall I pour it out for you, miss?' she asked.

'Yes, thank you,' said Eleanor.

The maid poured the water into a pretty porcelain bowl, then helped Eleanor to unfasten her dress so that she could wash herself in the lavender-scented water. Whilst she did so, the maid set a flatiron by the fire, and when it was hot enough she ironed Eleanor's gown.

The gown was not really suitable for evening wear, but still, that could not be helped. Eleanor dried herself on a fluffy towel and then slipped back into her dress. Now that it was ironed, it did not look too bad, she thought, as she surveyed herself critically in the cheval-glass. It might be rather old, but at least it was no longer wrinkled.

She sat down so that the maid could arrange her hair. The young girl unpinned it deftly, loosing it from its chignon and letting it cascade around Eleanor's shoulders. Then she took up a silver-backed hairbrush and brushed the brown locks until they shone. Finally, she twisted Eleanor's hair into a fashionable knot and pinned it neatly on top of her head.

'Thank you,' said Eleanor, nodding approvingly at the maid's handiwork.

Well, she was as clean and tidy as she could make herself, she thought as she examined the finished result. She left her room and went downstairs.

It was too early for dinner and the other guests, having more elaborate toilettes to make, were still in their rooms. She was relieved, for it would give her time to slip into the drawing-room and write a note to Arabella. Her absence would be prolonged, and she did not want her sister to worry. At the moment Arabella was staying with friends, but when she returned she would be concerned if Eleanor was not at home.

Eleanor crossed the hall and opened the door of the drawing-room. But no sooner had she stepped across the threshold than she realized she was not alone. There, with his foot on the fender, was the one person she did not want to see, the enigmatic Lord Silverton.

Despite herself, her eyes lingered on him. There was something about him that drew her gaze. It was not just that he was darkly handsome, although with his black hair, lean face, steely blue eyes and cleft chin he was undoubtedly that. It was something more. Was it because he was so perplexing? she wondered. She found herself wanting to know more about him. Such as, what could induce a wealthy nobleman to hold up a stagecoach? But then she told herself that the reason was unimportant. What *was* important was that Lord Silverton was dangerous, and it would not do for her to be alone with him.

She was about to slip soundlessly out of the

room again when, as if sensing her presence, he turned round. There was a tense moment. They stood looking at each other across the elegant furnishings and Aubusson carpet as though it was a battleground instead of a drawing-room.

Then, making no mention of their earlier encounter, he fixed her with his steely blue eyes and made her a slight bow. 'Miss Grantham,' he said politely.

What was going through his mind? she wondered. Did he know she had recognized him? Or did he suspect? Or was he satisfied that she had not? Had he expected her to denounce him? And how did he feel now that she hadn't? Did he feel safe? Or did he feel wary? She wished she knew.

His eyes never wavered. They held hers in a penetrating gaze. She had an urge to make an excuse and back out of the room, but to do so would be tantamount to admitting that she had recognized him, and that was something she did not want to do. A man who was capable of holding up a stagecoach was surely capable of resorting to violence if he felt his safety was threatened, and so she must pretend to accept him as just another of Lydia and Frederick's guests.

'Lord Silverton.' She returned his greeting, politely inclining her head.

'Won't you come in?' He took his foot from the fender. 'I'm sure the other guests will be down presently. It will not be long before dinner.'

She lingered by the door. There was something in the atmosphere that made her wary. Although his words were innocuous she had the feeling that he was testing her defences, probing her strengths and weaknesses, and that she must be on her guard.

Drawing herself up to her full height of five feet and six inches she did her best to appear calm and collected. 'Thank you,' she said, as she walked into the room.

She took a seat that was as far away from him as was politely possible, perching on the edge of an elegant Hepplewhite chair.

There was a strained silence.

Then he said searchingly, 'It must have been a shock for you, being held up by a highwayman this afternoon. I hope you were not too alarmed?'

She had not expected him to refer to the robbery, and wondered whether he was toying with her. Deciding in the end that he was trying to find out whether or not she had recognized him she turned her eyes to his and replied in the same cool tone, 'No.'

'Ah. Good. I'm pleased. I wouldn't like to think you had been afraid.'

You didn't care whether I was afraid or not. The angry words were on the tip of her tongue, and she had to bite them back. She saw his eyes sharpen, as though he sensed that she had been about to commit herself. The thought stiffened her spine. Mastering her emotion, she said instead, 'Fortunately not.'

She was determined not to give anything away, and to reply to his probing questions with only the most basic answers.

The clock ticked loudly on the mantelpiece.

As it did so, Eleanor found a new idea taking shape in her mind. If Lord Silverton was the highwayman, then that meant that he was now in possession of Mr Kendrick's case. Which meant that he might possibly be in possession of Arabella's letters. The idea made her see things, however unwillingly, in a different light. If she told him that she had recognized him, then all she had to do was to ask him if he had the letters. It was tempting. If he said that he had, then Arabella's problem was solved. But did she have the courage to ask him?

Or rather, did she have the recklessness?

Because that was what it would be, recklessness, to admit that she knew who he was.

She hesitated.

And yet if it meant that she could reclaim Arabella's letters without ever having to speak to Mr Kendrick, might it not be worth it?

Should she or shouldn't she? She found herself torn in two directions. But in the end, she realized that it came down to an even simpler question: who was she more afraid of, Mr Kendrick or Lord Silverton?

'Will you be staying with Lydia and Frederick for long?' Lord Silverton's voice cut across her musings.

She brought her wandering thoughts back to the present. 'No.' To her annoyance, her voice cracked on the word, betraying signs of her tension. She moistened her lips and then said, 'I am only staying the one night. I will be travelling onwards tomorrow.'

'A pity.' His tone of voice, however, did not go with the words. Indeed, it sounded as though he should have been saying, *Thank God!*

There was another silence.

Eleanor weighed up the arguments, and in the end she decided to speak. But just as she was about to ask the question the door opened and Mrs Benson entered the room.

Eleanor bit her lip in vexation. Couldn't the glamorous woman have waited another few minutes before coming downstairs?

Seeming to sense some of the tension in the room, Mrs Benson stopped short when she saw Eleanor and Lord Silverton, alone together. But her scowl was quickly replaced by a charming, if false, smile and she came forward in a cloud of expensive scent.

'Miss Grantham,' she purred. 'I didn't think you would be downstairs so soon. But as you have no evening dress to wear, I should have expected it. Not that it matters,' she added patronizingly. 'Your quaint little muslin looks charming, my dear.'

She gave Lord Silverton an arch smile, as if inviting him to ridicule Eleanor's gown, but instead he turned away.

Mrs Benson scowled.

Fortunately—for the atmosphere was becoming decidedly frosty—the door opened again, and Mrs Oliver entered with her daughter.

Making the most of the opportunity to extricate herself from the conversation, Eleanor went over to the escritoire and took up a quill. She pulled out some paper and began to compose her letter to Arabella.

Her mouth quirked as, in the background, she could hear Mrs Oliver regaling Lord Silverton with a list of Miss Oliver's many perfections. She could almost feel sorry for him! It seemed that every female in the house had set her cap at him. But would they have been so eager to attract his attention if they knew how he had spent his day? she wondered.

'And she sings divinely!' Mrs Oliver gushed. 'She is so obliging, that I am sure if you ask her for a song after dinner she will not disappoint you.'

'Mother!' said Miss Oliver in agonized tones. 'Please don't.'

'Nonsense, child. Lord Silverton would love

42

to hear you sing,' said her redoubtable mama. 'He has spent many long years in the army, and now that he is home again he is longing for some superior company. It is just a pity the Fairacres have no instrument, otherwise you could delight him with your playing as well.'

The other guests soon began to fill the drawing-room, until at last they were all assembled and dinner was announced.

'Oh, dear, and Frederick has not returned,' said Lydia as she organized her guests with their dinner partners. 'He was called away to investigate the hold-up and he hasn't yet come back. But we will not delay our dinner for him, he will probably be away for some time. Now, if we are all ready, I suggest we go in.'

Eleanor was relieved to find that she was to be taken into dinner by a pleasant young man named Mr Vernon. She had feared that she might have had to go in with Lord Silverton, but he was escorting Mrs Oliver and she breathed a sigh of relief. If she had had to put her hand on his arm it would have been an ordeal, and it was one she would rather not face. For some reason his touch had a profound effect on her, and given the circumstances it was not something she wanted to feel again.

Although it had been rather wonderful . . .

'It must have been alarming, having the coach stopped like that,' said Mr Vernon, as he handed Eleanor to her place at the table.

'Enough to give a young lady a fit of the vapours.'

'Now, really, Peter, let the poor girl sit down before you start quizzing her,' protested Lydia.

Eleanor glanced at Lord Silverton, wondering how he would react to talk of the robbery. Would it unsettle him? Or would he be unconcerned?

He appeared to be the latter. He was sitting at the table and seemed perfectly at ease, but even so she could feel a wave of tension emanating from him. Could anyone else feel it? she wondered. But a glance round the table showed her that they could not.

'I think it must have been wonderful!' said Miss Oliver, going slightly pink. She looked at Eleanor shyly. 'Was he *very* handsome?'

'Handsome,' snorted her mother, obviously annoyed that her daughter would dream of a highwayman when she had a perfectly good earl close at hand. 'You've been reading too many novels, my girl. Highwaymen aren't handsome. He was none too clean, as like as not, and had a mouthful of black teeth.'

Eleanor instinctively glanced towards Lord Silverton, and saw him give a wicked smile. She was almost tempted to smile as well. Fortunately the sound of a carriage pulling up in front of the house saved her from such folly.

'That must be Frederick now!' exclaimed Lydia, turning towards the window. 'Oh, good, I'm so glad he's home. It would have been too bad if this wretched business had robbed him of his dinner.'

A few minutes later, Frederick walked into the room. He greeted his guests warmly, apologizing for his absence. He was a good-looking man of middle years, with an air of dignity about him that befitted his role as the local magistrate. His black tail coat had a conservative cut and his cravat was simply arranged, whilst his knee-breeches and stockings had a solid, if slightly old-fashioned, air.

'And look, Frederick, here is Eleanor,' said Lydia, drawing Eleanor to his notice as he took his place at the head of the table.

Frederick was too polite to ask why Eleanor had suddenly appeared at his dinner table, and greeted her warmly. 'It is a pleasure to see you here, Eleanor. You are very welcome.'

'Eleanor will be staying with us overnight, and longer if I can persuade her,' Lydia explained. 'She was on the stagecoach, going to London to visit the modiste's, when it was held up, and by good fortune I encountered her at the coaching inn and insisted she come here for the night.'

'Quite right too,' said Frederick approvingly as the mulligatawny soup was brought in. 'It was a nasty business.' He turned to Eleanor. 'But it's one I hope you will be able to help us clear up. Strangely enough, I've had my men out looking for you for the last hour without having any idea whom I was looking for. The statements they took from the other passengers mentioned a young lady on the coach, but I never thought I'd discover her sitting at my own dinner table.'

There was a ripple of laughter, and an exclamation from Mrs Oliver of, 'Well I never!'

'But do tell us, Miss Grantham,' said Mrs Benson as the soup was served. 'What was it like?'

'Yes. Tell us, if you will,' said Frederick. He settled his napkin on his knee. 'It will be very useful to have your account. And then, if you don't mind, one of my men can make a written record of it in the morning.'

Eleanor felt her spirits sink. She had no wish to get involved, for the situation was extremely complicated, but she could hardly refuse to co-operate with Frederick.

'What I want to know is, what was the highwayman like?' asked Miss Oliver breathlessly.

Mrs Benson paused with her spoon half-way to her mouth and said, with a sideways glance at Lord Silverton, 'My guess is that he would look a lot like Silverton.'

Eleanor was startled. Did Mrs Benson know something? she wondered.

But no. Mrs Benson was simply being provocative, as her slanting glance in Lord Silverton's direction showed.

Lord Silverton seemed unconcerned,

making no more reply than by giving a sardonic smile. In fact, if Eleanor's gaze had not at that moment dropped to the table she would have believed that he was perfectly at ease. But her eyes happened to fall on his wineglass, and she saw that his knuckles, wrapped round the stem, were white.

As if feeling her eyes on him he looked up and said challengingly, 'Yes, tell us, Miss Grantham. What was the highwayman like?'

There was a sudden silence. Everyone at the table turned towards Eleanor.

He doesn't know whether I have recognized him, she realized with a moment of sudden clarity, and he wants to be sure. She was aware of standing on a threshold. This was the moment when she must decide whether or not to reveal Lord Silverton's identity. She must either declare that yes, there was a marked resemblance . . . that they were of the same height, they had the same eyes, the same hair . . . before revealing that Lord Silverton was the highwayman. Or hold her peace.

She was torn. On the one hand she did not want to let him get away with his crime. But on the other hand she had no proof, and besides, she was convinced there was more to the situation than met the eye.

And then there was the idea that had occurred to her in the drawing-room just before dinner: that, as Lord Silverton was the highwayman, he was now in possession of Mr

47

Kendrick's case, and therefore possibly also in possession of Arabella's letters. Which gave her another reason for not exposing him. She had decided before dinner that she would question him about the contents of the case, and she stood by her decision, for her loyalty to her sister outweighed all other concerns. That being so she could not denounce him, as she could not risk his being imprisoned before she had a chance to speak to him.

Eleanor looked straight ahead. 'He was nothing like Lord Silverton,' she said.

She felt a twinge of conscience, but she must learn to live with it, for the die was now cast.

In all this time Lord Silverton had not looked at her. But as she declared that the highwayman was nothing like him, he glanced at her and their eyes held. And then he looked away.

She had been unable to read his expression. Relief? Perhaps. Satisfaction? She did not know him well enough to be sure. Even so, she felt his tension ebb, and saw the colour return to his knuckles.

'What did he look like, then?' asked Frederick as he finished his soup. 'It would be helpful if you could give me a description. The ones I've got so far unfortunately aren't of much use. You'd think that seven people, all being held up by the same man, would give the same description,' he said with a sigh. 'But not a bit of it! I would value your account.'

'He was smaller than Lord Silverton—' Eleanor began.

'Oh, what a shame,' said Mrs Benson. 'I do so like the men I dream about to be tall.' She glanced again at Lord Silverton.

Lord Silverton's mouth curved in a mocking smile.

Eleanor took a deep breath. 'And his eyes were green.'

'Now that's a useful snippet,' said Frederick. 'How exactly do you know? No one else was able to give us any clear details.'

'I saw them when he—'

'Yes?'

All eyes were fixed on her.

'When he kissed my hand.'

'He kissed your hand? Oh, how romantic,' sighed Miss Oliver, clasping her hands together in a gesture of girlish delight.

'Don't be a fool, child,' snorted her mother. 'Romantic! Highwaymen aren't romantic. Thieves and robbers, that's what they are. No respect for other people's property, and shoot you as soon as look at you, so don't you forget it.'

Miss Oliver, duly chastened, relapsed into silence, but the look on her face showed that she had not abandoned her dreams, whatever her mother might say.

'And you, Miss Grantham? Did you find it romantic?' asked Lord Silverton, shooting her a devilish look.

A brief memory of the sparks that had flared between them when he had kissed her hand returned to disturb her, but she didn't intend to give him the satisfaction of knowing it.

'No,' she replied coolly, returning his gaze. 'As Mrs Oliver says, highwaymen are nothing but common thieves.'

His mouth gave a sardonic curl, but even so there was something annoyed in his glance and she had the satisfaction of knowing that she had given him a set-down.

'Is there anything else you can remember about him?' asked Frederick, as the plates were cleared away.

'I'm afraid not.'

'Hair colour?'

She shook her head. 'It was dark. I could not say for certain. Brownish.'

'Any scars, or distinguishing features?'

'I didn't see any.'

'And how about his build? He was short, you said, but was he slim? Stocky? Fat?'

Again Eleanor shook her head. 'He was wearing a cloak. It was blowing around him in the wind. I really couldn't say.'

Frederick nodded. 'Oh, well, it's not much to go on, but still, it's a help. And far better than any of the other descriptions we've been given. The clergyman on the coach said he looked like the devil—'

'Are you *sure* it wasn't you, Silverton?'

50

interposed Mrs Benson.

Lord Silverton gave a wicked smile. 'My estates are large enough to acquit me of the crime, I believe. A man of my fortune has no need to steal a few trinkets.'

There was general laughter.

'And a stout matron said he was definitely hunchbacked. There was another man in the coach, apparently, but we haven't been able to trace him yet.'

'I know who he was. He was a Mr Kendrick,' said Eleanor.

Lord Silverton shot her a sharp look.

Now why should he mind my knowing Mr Kendrick's name? she wondered. But she did not allow herself to wonder about it for long. The fact that Frederick was looking for Mr Kendrick was a matter of much more importance to her. If it turned out that Lord Silverton did not have the letters, then she would still need to find Mr Kendrick. On her own, it would be an almost impossible task. But if Frederick, in his capacity as the local magistrate, conducted a search for Mr Kendrick, he would have a good chance of success. He had a lot of manpower at his disposal, and he could ask detailed questions as to Mr Kendrick's whereabouts without anyone thinking it odd. Which meant that all Eleanor had to do, instead of looking for Mr Kendrick herself, was to wait until Frederick found him.

It was an unexpected bonus.

'Kendrick, you say?' Frederick was thoughtful.

'Yes.'

Frederick drummed his fingers on the table. 'I don't know the name. He's not one of our neighbours. A visitor, then, to these parts. But now that we know his name it shouldn't be too difficult to track him down. Not that I suppose there's anything he can tell us, but you never know.'

'He was met by a private carriage,' went on Eleanor. 'I saw him getting into it outside the inn,' she explained.

'Well, that is useful. There are only a few families round here who keep their own carriages. It will give us somewhere to start.'

'And now I suggest we let poor Eleanor eat her meal in peace,' said Lydia as she saw that Eleanor had not had a chance to start the delicious turbot that had just been served. 'She has hardly touched her food, and after all the excitement she must be starving.'

Eleanor was glad of the respite. She had much to occupy her as the succeeding courses were brought in, and she was pleased to be able to relapse into silence and listen to the rest of the guests without having to make conversation herself.

Uppermost in her mind was the problem of how she was going to be able to speak to Lord Silverton alone. Now that she had decided to ask him about the contents of the case she would need to speak to him privately. She was longing to know if the letters had been in Mr Kendrick's case. If so, she might soon hold them in her hands.

If not . . .

If not, she thought reluctantly, she would just have to go ahead with her original plan, and track down Mr Kendrick.

*　　*　　*

Had she recognized him or hadn't she?

That was the thought that plagued Lucien as he sat over the port. The ladies had withdrawn, and the gentlemen were engaged in a heated discussion on politics, so that his silence would not be noticed. Which gave him time to think over the perplexing problem.

It had been a bad moment for him when Lydia, returning from town, had announced Miss Grantham, and he had caught sight of her in a mirror. If not for the fact that he had had his back to her he feared his shock would have shown. Fortunately, he had had time to school his features before greeting her, but there was no doubt about it, her arrival had come as a blow.

As he looked into the wineglass that he held in his hand he saw, not the ruby liquid, but Miss Grantham's image. He should have known better than to let her get so close to him when he had held up the coach, but at the time there had seemed little risk. He had been masked, and swathed in an enveloping black cloak, and besides, he had not expected to see her again. Still, it had been careless of him. The worst of it was, that it had not been necessary. If he had been able to persuade himself that he had needed someone to collect the valuables in order to make the robbery seem convincing, and that he had chosen Miss Grantham because she had been the least frightened of all the passengers, he would have had little with which to reproach himself. But if he was honest, he knew that it was more than that.

He remembered her as he had first seen her on the coach, looking shabby and worn in her old, dowdy clothes. He had taken her for a governess or a companion. But then his glance had wandered over her face and instead of dropping her eyes she had met his gaze. There had been strength in that look, and a calm, collected courage which had intrigued him.

It was strange that she should have compelled his attention. She had an ordinary face, and he would not normally have given her a second glance. If he had he seen her at a ball or a soirée he would have scarcely noticed her, with her nondescript brown hair and ordinary brown eyes. She had nothing to mark her out as being unusual.

And yet her eyes were not quite brown.

They were closer to hazel, with a golden tinge that lightened the brown and brought it to life. He had noticed it particularly when he had grasped her hand . . . Which he should not have done. But, he reminded himself, she had been trying to take his pistol at the time.

An unwilling smile lifted the corner of his mouth. She had certainly been audacious! It had been a bold move, and one which might have succeeded, if she had she been a little quicker and he had been a little less alert.

His smile vanished. In which case the results could have been disastrous.

He should have left it there, he told himself, and no harm would have been done. However, admiring her audacity, he had lifted her hand to his lips. His eyes smouldered as he thought of the effect his kiss had unleashed. It had been both intense and unexpected, and it had caught him off guard. He had not expected anything so overpowering. And yet even that might not have been so bad. But why, in the name of all sanity, when Lydia had introduced them, had he kissed her hand again? It had been little short of madness.

He found his motives difficult to understand. Recklessness? He did not think so. A desire to see if she had recognized him? Possibly: by kissing her hand he had given her every opportunity of discovering that he and the highwayman were one and the same—a rash act in one sense, and yet in another sense a necessary one, for if she had guessed his identity, then it was better that he should know that at once.

But had she guessed it?

For a moment he had thought so. He had tensed, waiting for her to denounce him. But she had not done so.

Why not? Why had she not revealed his identity? he asked himself. It was a puzzle. And he didn't like puzzles. Especially not when he was involved in a dangerous plot to retrieve stolen military documents.

He had tried to draw her out later that evening, when he had encountered her in the drawing-room, but their conversation had been inconclusive. He had thought she had been about to reveal something, but then Mrs Benson had walked into the room and the moment had been lost.

Frederick's arrival had provided another difficult moment. He had been so tense that he had feared the stem of his wineglass would snap, particularly when the conversation had turned to the subject of the hold-up. Mrs Benson's questions had been a nuisance, but he could have dealt with them: her arch looks and inviting smiles had made it obvious to everyone what lay behind them. But Frederick's questions had been of a different kind. One word from Miss Grantham could have exposed him. And yet she had not said the word.

Why not?

It was possible that she had not recognized him, but he didn't believe it. There had been something in the look she had given him that convinced him she knew. Why, then, had she not spoken?

It was a puzzle. Miss Grantham, instead of growing easier to understand, was growing more intriguing with every passing hour.

'. . . do you think, Silverton?' asked Sir Thomas Nugent.

His attention was recalled to the conversation. He had no idea what he was being asked and threw off the rest of his port to give himself time to think.

'The war with France won't be over in a hurry, whatever you say, Nugent,' said Mr Vernon, 'especially not now that Napoleon's divorced Josephine and married his new wife, Marie Louise. What a way to strengthen his position in Europe, by marrying an Austrian archduchess! Not bad for the son of a lawyer. You can say what you like about Napoleon, but he has grand ambitions.'

'The Austrians didn't like it,' pointed out Sir Thomas. 'They only went along with it because they had to, but all the same, they didn't want to let him have Marie Louise.'

'But they *did* have to let him have her, that's the point, eh, Silverton?' asked Mr Vernon.

Lucien put down his glass and gave his full attention to his fellow guests. 'The war's far from over. We've still got a long battle on our hands,' he agreed.

'But we'll beat him?' asked Sir Thomas Nugent a trifle anxiously. He was a foppish gentleman, and the idea of losing the war evidently worried him.

Lucien nodded. 'I hope so. But Napoleon is going to be with us for a long time to come.'

*   *   *

Sitting over coffee with the other ladies in the drawing-room, Eleanor was finding conversation something of a strain. The day had been tiring, and she was looking forward to an early night.

'You look tired, Eleanor,' said Lydia.

'I am,' Eleanor admitted. She put down her cup. 'If you don't mind, I think I will retire.'

'Not at all. I think it's a good idea. You must be exhausted after the journey, to say nothing of all the worry of the hold-up. I know I am always fatigued after travelling on the stagecoach.'

Eleanor bid the other ladies goodnight and then, leaving them to their chatter, she left the room. Climbing the branching staircase she turned towards her bedchamber—and then started to have misgivings. The panelled walls were familiar, but surely the pictures lining them were showing scenes she had not seen before? The paintings had been of landscapes

58

on her way down to dinner but now they had changed into portraits. There was only one explanation. Her thoughts being on other things, she must have taken a wrong turn.

Up ahead of her she saw a maid. She was just about to ask for directions when the girl vanished into one of the bedrooms. A minute later the housekeeper appeared and followed the maid into the room.

'Hurry up, girl,' Eleanor heard the housekeeper say. 'As soon as you've turned down Lord Silverton's bed I want you to help me with Miss Grantham's room. It's still not ready, and she'll be retiring soon.'

Lord Silverton's room? thought Eleanor. She must have wandered into the bachelor wing by mistake. She was about to turn round and retrace her steps when she paused. Here was an opportunity for her to find out if the letters had been in Mr Kendrick's case, without putting herself in a vulnerable position. She had discovered where Lord Silverton's room was, and discovered it at a time when he was safely downstairs. If she slipped inside and looked in the case herself, she would not need to let him know that she had recognized him.

Could she bring herself to go into Lord Silverton's bedroom? Gently raised as she was, she did not like the idea. But her sister's happiness was at stake, and she knew she had to do it.

By and by the housekeeper left the room, followed by the maid. Eleanor waited for them to disappear round the corner of the corridor, then slipped inside. It was dark. The only light came from the moon shining in through the window. Giving her eyes a moment to adjust to the gloomy conditions, she moved further into the room. She was in luck. The case was on a mahogany console table next to the bed. She went over to it. She pressed the catches and to her relief the lid sprang up. Lord Silverton had evidently picked the lock. She opened the case to its full extent . . . and then felt a wave of dismay. It was empty.

Had the letters ever been in the case? she wondered. Perhaps they had, and Lord Silverton had removed them. She was just about to light a candle and examine the room when she became aware of footsteps in the corridor. She closed the case quickly and turned round, only to see the door handle turning. She froze. And then the door swung open . . . to reveal Lord Silverton.

Eleanor's heart missed a beat. Unwillingly, her eyes were drawn to his face, with its olive skin drawn firmly across his cheekbones. It was a handsome face, but also a harsh one, made even harsher by the blackness of his hair and the steeliness of his eyes. His jaw was firm, and his mouth was set in a grim line.

'My dear Miss Grantham.' The air crackled dangerously. 'What a pleasant surprise.'

CHAPTER THREE

Eleanor's heart began to hammer in her chest. She tried to speak, but her mouth was dry and no sound came out. She licked her lips.

'I expect you're wondering what I'm doing here,' she said at last, to break the taut silence.

'It's not uncommon for a woman to visit my room . . .' he said speculatively.

Eleanor was almost stung into making a scathing comment, but remembered at the last minute that she could not let the words pass her lips. If she revealed that she was not there for that purpose, then she would have to explain why she was there; and that was something she was not yet ready to do.

'. . . although not usually innocent young virgins,' he finished dangerously.

Eleanor swallowed.

'Yes, well. There is a very good explanation,' she said, playing for time. She rubbed her palms together and was mortified to discover that they had become damp.

'There had better be.'

His tone was bland, but there was menace beneath the surface. She was suddenly conscious of the fact that she was alone with him, and a shiver washed over her from head to foot.

'I . . . lost my way,' she said. Which was the

truth, if not the whole truth. 'I was trying to make my way back to my room after dinner but I must have taken a wrong turning on the stairway,' she hurried on. 'I found myself in a strange part of the house—'

'So, finding yourself at my door, you naturally decided to enter my room?'

She felt her courage sink still further. 'Yes . . . no . . . that is to say . . .'

He walked towards her. Then he lifted her chin, so that she was forced to meet his gaze. 'That is to say?' he prompted her silkily.

'That is to say, I . . . wanted to find my bearings.'

'Ah.' His voice was gentle. But the finger lifting her chin was joined by his thumb and he held her chin in a suddenly pincerlike grip. His voice sharpened. 'And how did you intend to do that?'

'I . . .' Without realizing it, she held her breath.

His expression suddenly hardened, and his voice became harsh. 'Tell me, Miss Grantham. What were you *really* doing in my room?'

She gulped down some much-needed air. Then she straightened her shoulders. It was obvious she was not going to be able to fool Lord Silverton. She had no choice but to tell him the truth.

'Very well. I will tell you. Just as soon as you let go of me.' His eyes glittered, and he held her chin for another minute. But then his hand dropped.

She gave a sigh of relief . . . although for some reason she missed the touch of his strong fingers. She shook the disturbing thought away. Then, summoning her courage, she said, 'May I sit down?'

Glancing at the chairs that flanked the fireplace, he said, 'Very well.'

Eleanor seated herself in one of the wing chairs. It was fortunate she did so, for as she lowered herself into the chair she felt her legs begin to shake. The tension of the last few minutes had caught up with her, and she was glad she no longer had to stand. She gave herself a few moments to steady her nerve. She arranged her skirts so that she would seem busy, and so that he would not guess how nervous she was. But just as she plucked up the courage to speak Lord Silverton closed the door and she started up, nervous again.

'If anyone sees you in my room, your reputation will be damaged,' he said by way of explanation, following her eyes to the closed door. 'And I'm sure you wouldn't want that.'

Eleanor glanced at his face, trying to read his expression. Did he mean it? she wondered. Had he really closed the door for her protection? Or had he done it to trap her? She had no way of knowing. But deciding to take his words at face value, at least for the moment, she resumed her seat.

He took a taper from the mantelpiece and

thrust it into the fire. Once it was glowing, he used it to light the candles that stood on the small fireside table, and those in the wall sconces. The light blossomed, filling the dark corners with a gentle glow. He replaced the taper and leant his elbow against the mantelpiece.

Eleanor tried to ignore his eyes, which were fixed on her in the most penetrating way. She took a deep breath and then began.

'On leaving the drawing-room I climbed the stairs, intending to retire for the night,' she said, 'but I must have taken the wrong branch. I began to realize that the pictures on the wall were portraits instead of landscapes. By the time I knew for certain that I was lost I found myself outside your room. I knew it was yours because I heard the housekeeper telling the maid to hurry with Lord Silverton's room,' she explained. 'Realizing I was in the bachelor wing I was about to turn back and retrace my steps, when I thought better of it, because . . .' It was now or never. She must decide whether or not to reveal that she knew who he was. She took a deep breath. '. . . because you have something I want.'

His eyebrows lifted. 'So. I have something you want.' He gave her a searching look, then his lips curved in a wicked smile. 'Perhaps you are not so innocent after all.'

He reached out one hand and, closing it round her wrist, dragged her to her feet. He pulled her to him, encircling her with his strong arms whilst his eyes traced the line of her brows, her eyes, and her nose, before dropping to her lips . . .

She was about to pull away from him, but his hand reached out and cupped the back of her head and she tingled from head to foot. His dark head bent towards her and her face turned towards his of its own accord. She could feel the hot whisper of his breath against her skin as his mouth approached hers. It caressed her like a hot wind blowing across the desert. It blew across her lips . . . and suddenly she knew that if she did not break free of the spell that bound her she would surrender herself to him.

She made an effort to step back, but before her unwilling body could respond his lips closed over hers. Her mouth came alive with new and completely unknown sensations that set her body trembling. Without realizing what she was doing she began to respond, her mouth moving under his with a passion that matched his own. He crushed her to him, pulling her ever more tightly into his embrace. It was a joining of two people in a way she had never even imagined, and she gave herself up to the new and mesmerizing sensations, living for the moment, unable to think of anything else.

And then his mouth left hers.

After a moment of confusion she began to

return to reality, and as he pulled away from her she flushed scarlet, overcome with confusion.

What have I done? she thought agonizingly. She had behaved unforgivably, and did not know what she had been thinking of. How could she have so far forgotten herself that she would allow a man, an almost complete stranger, to kiss her—in his bedchamber, of all places—and even worse, respond? And, worse again, a man who was responsible for holding up a stagecoach?

Trying to salvage the situation as best she could, she smoothed the folds of her crushed muslin whilst she steadied her nerves, then said, 'That is not what I meant.' Her voice was ragged. Uneven. Coming in quick, short gasps.

'No?' One eyebrow rose mockingly. His eyes roved over her flushed cheeks and parted lips.

She fought down her blushes and hurried on. 'I came into the room . . .' She stopped to steady herself. Feeling her blushes subside, she lifted her chin and said—as calmly as she could—'I came to your room because I wanted to look inside the case.'

She broke off. A deathly silence had suddenly filled the room. At the words *the case* it was as though everything had stopped. Lord Silverton's expression was frozen, and she was unable to move.

Then Lord Silverton's expression changed.

66

The mockery left his eyes, and they became hard and glittering. His jaw clenched, and his muscles tightened under his clothes. And what magnificent muscles they were, she thought involuntarily, as her eyes were drawn to them against her will. They were sculpted, their shape clearly defined beneath the superb cut of his garments. As her gaze wandered from his powerful shoulders and well-shaped arms to the hard muscles of his legs she found herself thinking of a marble statue she had seen of a hero from Greek mythology . . . before blushing deeply, because the statue had been naked. And confronted as she was by Lord Silverton's masculine contours, that thought set her imagination spiralling down new and perilously disturbing channels.

But she must not think of it. She must put all such unseemly thoughts out of her mind. She was alone in the room of a dangerous man, and she needed her wits about her. In fact, right now he seemed more dangerous than ever. Her mention of the case had caused a change in him. It had made him tense. Like a panther about to spring.

Well, she had committed herself now.

'And which particular case are you talking about?' he asked. There was an air of restraint about him that spoke of an inner battle and an iron will, but there was an ominous edge to his voice that made Eleanor shiver. 'My dressing-case, perhaps?' he enquired.

The tension that had filled the room made Eleanor's head spin. Still, this was no time to lose her nerve. She lifted her chin and looked him directly in the eye. 'No. Not your dressing-case.' She paused. Then, gathering her courage, she said, 'The case you took from Mr Kendrick.'

A wave of danger rolled through the room. Large and looming, Lord Silverton was a palpable presence, and she was suddenly filled with doubt. She should not have shown her hand. She should not have revealed to him that she knew beyond a shadow of a doubt that he was the highwayman. It had been a huge mistake.

He was still reining himself in. Still holding himself in check. 'I, Miss Grantham?' he asked dangerously.

She swallowed. Then said, with as much courage as she could muster, 'Yes, Lord Silverton. You.'

They looked at each other for long moments.

Bit by bit, some of the unbearable tension began to ebb.

'You intrigue me, Miss Grantham,' he said at last. 'First of all you show no fear when I hold up the coach you are travelling on, and then, even though you recognize me, you make no exclamation when you are unexpectedly confronted with me at the local magistrate's house.'

68

She breathed a sigh of relief. At least he had not exploded. Still, she knew she must not drop her guard. Not even for a minute.

'You don't deny it, then?' she asked boldly, though inside she was feeling anything but bold. 'That you are the highwayman?'

He smiled. It would have broken the tension if it had not revealed his predatory white teeth.

'What would be the point?' he returned. 'You have obviously recognized me. Besides, reactions as violent as the one that took place between us do not happen every day.'

She felt a shiver wash over her as her body recalled that reaction: a force so powerful it had shaken her entire frame.

'I can't help wondering, though,' he went on thoughtfully, 'why you protected me. You had only to say the word and I would have been arrested.'

She shook her head. 'I doubt it. I had no proof. And you were obviously a man of some consequence. Besides—'

'Yes?' he prompted her.

She balled her hands into fists. 'I need you.' She hurried on, before he had a chance to misunderstand her again. 'If you had been arrested, I would never have known what was in the case.'

'Ah, yes. We are back to the case.' The tension was back in him, and the air of menace that had surrounded him earlier returned. 'So tell me, Miss Grantham, just why do you want to see inside Mr Kendrick's case?'

Well, she might as well tell him. It was what she was here for, after all. She took a deep breath. 'Because I want to find the letters.'

'Letters?' Did she imagine it, or was he surprised? Either way, some of the wariness seemed to leave him. 'What kind of letters?' he asked.

She steeled herself. 'Love letters. I was . . . hoping . . . to get them back.'

'Are you telling me Kendrick had stolen some *love letters* from you?' asked Lord Silverton with a sudden smile, although why he should be smiling she did not know. For some reason she could not fathom, he seemed to find it amusing, as though he had expected her to say something completely different.

'Not m—yes,' she finished. She had been going to say, *not me*, but changed her mind at the last minute. She did not want to mention Arabella—the fewer people who knew about her sister's indiscretion the better—and decided it would be as well to let him think the letters were hers. 'And I wanted to know if the letters were in the case. They're not there now,' she continued, 'but I need to know: were they there when you took it from Mr Kendrick?'

His eyes regarded hers searchingly, as if trying to ascertain the truth of what she was saying. She had no idea what he decided. 'I am sorry to disappoint you,' he replied at last. 'But no. There were no letters.'

Eleanor's face fell.

But she quickly recovered herself. 'Then I have a proposition to put to you.'

'Miss Grantham, you are full of surprises.'

She regarded him suspiciously, having the uncomfortable feeling he was mocking her. But instead, there was a light of admiration in his eyes.

When she did not speak, he said, 'Go on.'

'Very well. My proposition is this. I would like you to steal the letters for me.'

His eyebrows shot up. 'And just when I thought I could not be surprised any further,' he said under his breath.

'You have undertaken one robbery,' she said, nettled by his reaction. 'What is so different about undertaking another?'

'Everything. I held up the coach for . . . a wager. It is not something I am in the habit of doing.'

Her disappointment showed.

He looked at her thoughtfully for a minute, then said, 'If you have any sense you will forget about the letters. Mr Kendrick is not a pleasant man. He is mixed up in a number of unsavoury enterprises and he will not hesitate to harm you if you get in his way. You have no marriage forthcoming . . .' He broke off and looked at her quizzically.

'No.'

'In that case, the letters can do little

more than cause you some temporary embarrassment. Forget about them, Miss Grantham. Mr Kendrick is an evil man. You would do well to leave him alone.'

Forgetting about the letters was, for Eleanor, out of the question, but as it was clear she was going to get no help from Lord Silverton she simply inclined her head. 'In that case, I will not keep you.' She began to walk towards the door.

His arm rose and barred her way. She looked up at him, but in the candlelight his face was shadowed and she could not read his expression. For a moment she thought he was not going to let her pass. But then he stood aside.

'Good night, Miss Grantham,' he said softly.

'Good night, Lord Silverton,' she returned.

Once out of the room, she gave a huge sigh of relief. Thank goodness that is over, she thought as the door closed behind her. Gathering her wits she retraced her steps along the corridor and down the stairs. Then, concentrating on which way she was going, she returned to her own room. Once inside, she leant back against the door. She felt as though she had just fought a battle, instead of having just held a conversation, though undeniably a menacing one.

As she began to recover her composure, her eyes wandered round the room. The bed was turned down, and looked inviting. A nightgown had been laid out on the pillow and a note was laid on top of it. She went over to the bed and saw that the note was from Lydia.

I thought you might need this. Sleep well! it read.

She smiled. It was typical of Lydia to think of her, and the nightgown was much appreciated.

She put the note on the bedside table, then rang the bell for the maid. The young girl soon arrived and helped her to undress, unfastening her stays and putting her clothes neatly away. Then Eleanor slipped into bed.

As she did so she told herself that, first thing in the morning, she would be on her way. No matter how difficult her confrontation with Mr Kendrick might prove to be, she was convinced it could not be as nerve-racking as her encounter with Lord Silverton had been.

He was one person she did not want to see again!

CHAPTER FOUR

The following morning Eleanor woke early. After dressing quickly, she went down to breakfast. The sooner she found out where Mr Kendrick was, the sooner she would be on her way.

She hesitated as she reached the bottom of

the stairs. If Lord Silverton was in the dining-room . . . She shook the thought away. Then opening the door she went in. To her relief, the only person present was Frederick.

'Good morning,' said Frederick.

'Good morning.'

Eleanor seated herself at the magnificent mahogany table, whilst one of the servants brought her a cup of chocolate and a selection of hot rolls.

Eleanor took a sip of her chocolate, and then said nonchalantly, 'Your enquiries are going well, I hope? You have managed to find Mr Kendrick?'

She wanted to find out as much as possible about Mr Kendrick, without Frederick becoming suspicious, and a general question seemed the best way to do it.

On arriving she had reconsidered asking Frederick for his help and advice in the affair, but she had decided against the idea. Not only would it spare Arabella's blushes, but Eleanor knew that if she told him about the matter he would be sure to want to deal with it himself, and that was something she did not want him to do. Without any proof against Mr Kendrick there would be nothing he could do in his capacity as magistrate, and if he went to see Mr Kendrick on her behalf as a private gentleman, she was afraid that, as he was such a forceful man, he might antagonize the blackmailer. If that happened, Mr Kendrick might take his revenge by sending the letters to Charles's family. Reluctantly, she decided she must deal with the matter herself.

Frederick seemed to see nothing unusual in her question, and replied with perfect good humour. 'In a manner of speaking. My men checked all the houses in the neighbourhood with private carriages, and at last traced Mr Kendrick to the Seftons' home. Unfortunately, Mr Kendrick had already left. He only called on Mr Sefton for an hour or so on a matter of business yesterday evening and then retired to the inn, where he spent the night before travelling on to London.'

'London?' queried Eleanor: so he *was* going to London after all.

'Yes. He has a house in Pall Mall.'

Better and better, thought Eleanor; for although she did not relish seeing Mr Kendrick again, she was pleased to know his address.

'How do you know?' she asked curiously. 'Did Mr Sefton tell you so?'

'No. He only knew that Mr Kendrick had a house in London, not where it was. But we had a piece of luck. We found Mr Kendrick's card-case with the other things we recovered from the robbery.'

'I didn't know anything had been found,' said Eleanor in surprise. This was news to her.

'Oh, yes. Practically everything, by the look of it, although we shan't know for sure until

75

we've spoken to all the passengers. It seems the highwayman must have dropped his saddle-bags in his hurry to get away; they were found not far from the place where the coach was held up. It's a small consolation, I know, but it's good to know the blackguard didn't profit from his crime.'

Eleanor said nothing, but privately she put a different interpretation on events. She believed that Lord Silverton had deliberately dropped the saddle-bags so that the stolen goods could be returned to their owners. It would certainly fit in with his story about holding up the coach for a wager.

Unthinkingly, she crumbled her roll between her fingers. She still found it difficult to believe that Lord Silverton would indulge in such a childish prank, but she could think of no more satisfactory explanation for his behaviour. It was a puzzle in a whole jumble of puzzles about this enigmatic and dangerous man.

She turned her thoughts, with difficulty, back to Mr Kendrick. 'Will you be sending someone down to London to return Mr Kendrick's things?' she asked nonchalantly as she took another sip of chocolate. She had no wish to bump into one of Frederick's men, and wanted to know what Frederick's actions were going to be.

'No,' said Frederick. He spread a generous helping of marmalade on his toast. 'I don't have enough men for that. I've written to him and asked him to let me know exactly what he has lost, and once I've made sure I've got everything I'll invite him to collect his things the next time he visits the area. Which reminds me, if I could ask you to let me know exactly what you have lost? Then I can make sure that, if it has been found, it will be returned.'

'I was lucky. He took nothing.' Fortunately, as Lydia was not present, she did not have to answer any awkward questions about a supposedly-missing valise. 'In the meantime, I wonder if I could ask you to frank a letter for me?' She took the letter out of her reticule. 'I've written to Arabella to tell her that I will be delayed, and I would like her to find the letter waiting for her when she gets home. Otherwise she will worry if she returns from her friend's house and finds that I am not there.'

'That's a good idea,' said Frederick approvingly. 'Arabella has enough to worry about at the moment. She will be all in a jitter over the wedding.' He took the letter. 'I'll see that it catches the mail.'

Eleanor thanked him. 'And do you happen to know the time of the next coach for London?' she asked, as he tucked the letter in his pocket.

'I rather think Lydia was hoping to persuade you to stay for a few days,' he remarked. 'It will be a great pity if you have to leave us so soon, especially as you have only just arrived.'

Before Eleanor could reply the door opened, and Lydia entered the room. She was looking fresh and elegant in a high-waisted cambric gown.

'What's that?' she asked, having overheard the last part of Frederick's conversation. She turned to Eleanor. 'You are surely not leaving us already?'

'I'm afraid I must,' said Eleanor.

In any other circumstances she would have loved to stay. But she had pressing matters to attend to. And besides, she did not want to see Lord Silverton again.

Lydia's face fell. 'Oh, but I had been so looking forward to having you with us for a few days. Still, I suppose I can understand it,' she went on with a sigh. 'You will not want to leave Arabella on her own just now, and you must be wanting to sort out your new gown as quickly as possible so that you can be getting home.' She glanced at the ormolu clock on the mantelpiece. 'The next coach will be leaving in just over an hour. That should give you plenty of time to finish your breakfast and ready yourself for the journey. I think I will come with you into town.'

'But your guests,' protested Eleanor, not wanting to make difficulties for her kindly hostess.

'Most of them will still be in bed,' said Lydia practically. 'I have one or two purchases I need to make, and besides, it will allow me to spend a little extra time with you, so that you can tell me all about the wedding plans.' She raised her eyebrows. 'I want to hear all about Arabella's gown!'

Eleanor shook her head. 'I am sworn to secrecy!' she said with a smile.

'Then I will just have to wait until the wedding to see it,' said Lydia. 'Oh, I am so looking forward to it. It will be the event of the year. To think of little Arabella marrying a future duke! What a wonderful occasion it will be.'

Eleanor finished her breakfast and gathered her few belongings together before meeting Lydia in the hall.

The two ladies went outside. The carriage had been brought round and a footman opened the door. They stepped into the carriage and settled themselves comfortably, then Lydia knocked on the floor with her parasol and the carriage pulled away.

They soon reached the nearby town, and Eleanor transferred to the stagecoach. With a fond farewell and one last cry of, 'Make sure it's a pretty dress,' ringing in her ears Eleanor took her seat, and then she was on her way to London.

*   *   *

Going down to breakfast, Lucien was relieved

to discover that Miss Grantham had already left the house. She had given him a number of anxious moments and he was glad that he would not have to see her again. And yet it was not just because of the anxious moments that he was relieved to discover she had left. It was also because of the feelings she had stirred inside him. He was used to women of every type—or so he had thought. But Eleanor had been unique. She had not simpered at him in the manner of the débutantes who haunted society's ballrooms. Nor had she flirted with him, or given him arch looks, as the older and more experienced women he came across liked to do. Instead she had regarded him as a person; a man who could be argued with, reasoned with, even remonstrated with. When she had stood up to him on the highway he had been intrigued by her attitude, and impressed. She had neither trembled nor quaked, and she had told him what she thought of him—in no uncertain terms! For an earl who was used to being courted it made a refreshing change.

But it was when she had continued to treat him in the same manner, even when she had discovered his rank, that his interest had been firmly caught. She did not then start to simper at him, or even use her knowledge of his masquerade to coerce him into matrimony— something a number of young so-called ladies of his acquaintance, ably aided and abetted by their matchmaking mamas, would have had no hesitation in doing. Instead she had continued to stand up to him, and the sensation had been surprisingly enjoyable.

And yet for all that she had her flaws. Not least of which was her willingness to risk her neck by consorting with an evil piece of goods like Kendrick, just to retrieve some compromising letters.

It had been an unsettling moment for him when he had heard her mention Mr Kendrick's name, and he had wondered what she knew about the man. He had even considered the possibility that she could have been one of Kendrick's accomplices, particularly when he had found her in his room. But then he had discovered that she was looking for love-letters, and he had been relieved. For some reason that he did not fully understand he did not want her to be his enemy.

Even so, he couldn't understand why she had been so determined to retrieve the letters. She didn't love her correspondent, of that he was sure. She had kissed *him* too passionately for that. True, she had been out of her depth when he had taken her into his arms, and obviously innocent. But when he had kissed her she had responded to him as only an unattached woman could do. She had given herself completely, and for the few moments he had held her in his arms, she had been his.

A thoughtful smile crossed his face. She was

not a great beauty, but still her response had enlivened him more than a similar response from a beautiful woman would have done. Beautiful women were ten a penny. Women with courage and character—they were rare indeed. In fact, until he had met Eleanor, he had not known they existed.

The realization was strangely unsettling. It made him think of—but no. He was too young to set up his nurseries. Besides, he was involved in a dangerous and difficult mission, and he could not afford to lose his concentration. Miss Grantham had left Fairacres Park. She would go to London, visit the modiste's, then return home again. And he would dismiss her from his thoughts.

But he had the unsettling feeling it was going to be easier decided upon than accomplished.

In the meantime, he must make his excuses to Lydia and Frederick. His visit to Fairacres Park was going to have to be curtailed.

*   *   *

'Mr Kendrick.'

Eleanor, newly arrived in London, was holding an imaginary conversation with the blackmailer. She was sitting in the back of a hackney cab which was rattling its way through the streets towards Mr Kendrick's house in Pall Mall. 'Mr Kendrick,' she began again, 'I

have come to speak to you about Arabella's—
Miss Arabella Grantham's—letters. You have
demanded a thousand guineas from her, but
you must know she does not have so much
money. I have fifty guineas here. Will you not
give me the letters in return? Consider this. If
you show them to her fiancé you will only
arouse his hostility, and the hostility of a
future duke is not something to be taken
lightly. If, on the other hand, you return the
letters to me you will have fifty guineas and
you will spare yourself the anger of an
influential man.'

She frowned. Would that work? Possibly.
But somehow she didn't believe it.

She tried again.

'Mr Kendrick, you are mistaken in thinking
that my sister is clever. She's as helpless as a
child. There is no possibility of her finding a
thousand guineas. She would certainly never
ask Charles for the money, and there is no
other manner in which she could possibly get
it.'

She sighed. No, that did not sound right
either. Whatever she said, she did not think
Mr Kendrick would take any notice of her.
Still, she must try. If she tried, she at least had
a chance of succeeding, whereas if she didn't,
she would have no chance at all.

She was saved from further attempts to find
the right words as the hackney cab turned into
Pall Mall.

At last, she thought, I've arrived.

'Where did you say you wanted to be?' called the driver.

'This will do very well,' said Eleanor, who did not want the carriage to pull up directly in front of the house. 'You may stop here.'

The driver slowed the cab and as soon as it stopped, Eleanor stepped out. Having paid her fare she proceeded to the right address, which she had carefully noted down. The house formed a marked contrast to the run-down house she had visited on the outskirts of Bath. That, she now guessed, had been a business address, a house Mr Kendrick used solely for plying his dubious trade. This was in all likelihood where he lived. It was a splendid gentleman's residence. Brightly-polished brasses gleamed on the door, and the windows shone like mirrors. Everything about it exuded an air of wealth.

As she arranged the folds of her shabby cloak, Eleanor felt a moment of doubt. Would she be admitted to such a grand house? she wondered. Well, there was no use in delaying. She must just get on with it and hope for the best.

Straightening her spine, she resolutely approached the front door. She lifted the lion's-head knocker and let it drop, then she stood with bated breath, waiting for an answer. But nothing happened.

Thinking she must not have knocked hard

enough she lifted the lion's head again and this time brought it down firmly in a series of loud raps. As she gave the last, determined, knock she was surprised to feel the door give a little.

She drew back her hand, startled. Why had the door swung open a crack? Had it already been ajar? Perhaps. Even so, it seemed odd. She stood and waited, expecting a butler or a liveried footman to appear at any moment and ask her what her business was. But still no one came.

She had come too far now to turn back, however, and after waiting for another minute she decided to go in. Cautiously she pushed the door wide. It revealed a palatial hall. She gasped in awe. She had never seen its equal. Blackmailing was obviously a lucrative business.

The hall was dominated by a magnificent staircase, which swept upwards to a dizzying height. Above it, a glass dome was set into the roof, flooding the hall with daylight.

Her eyes travelled down again, taking in the costly gilded furniture and *objets d'art* that were artistically arranged. Marble columns supported Sévres vases; inlaid console tables held ormolu clocks. Classical pieces, brought back from the Continent, shimmered in the sunlight.

It was magnificent, thought Eleanor. Before reminding herself that it was built on ill-gotten gains. No doubt Arabella's thousand guineas, should she have been able to produce that sum, would have provided more masterpieces for the already crowded walls.

The thought sobered Eleanor. Taking her eyes away from the dazzling splendour, she looked about her for some sign of life. But there was nothing. There should have been a footman at least, but the hall was empty.

Had Mr Kendrick perhaps not arrived? But the knocker had been on the door, and that indicated he was in town. It was all very curious.

She moved forward. She tried to go quietly but she could not prevent her footsteps from echoing as she crossed the marble floor. She shivered, and pulled her cloak more closely about herself. There was something eerie about the silent house, and she felt the small hairs rise on the back of her neck.

If there was anyone at home, they would most probably be in the drawing-room. Knowing that it would be found on the first floor she set foot on the stairs. She looked up, her eyes travelling over the banister to the landing above in an effort to discover some sign of life, but still she could see no one.

Fighting down an irrational fear she began to climb. The stairs were broad and shallow. Once at the top, she went along the landing and pushed open the first door she came to. It revealed a sumptuously decorated ante-room. Mr Kendrick had spared no expense when it came to furnishing and decorating his house. An Aubusson carpet covered the floor. Brocaded sofas vied with gilded chairs for attention. A large chandelier hung from the ceiling, and the ceiling itself was painted with a large picture of Zeus.

But still there was no sign of Mr Kendrick.

She went into the next room. It was splendidly decorated, but had a different character from the rest of the house. This was a place to work. A large mahogany desk was set at one side, with a leather-upholstered chair pushed up next to it. The walls were covered with bookcases . . . and the room had been ransacked.

Eleanor's eyes ran over the jumble and confusion in dismay. The drawers had been wrenched out of the desk and turned upside down, their contents scattered all over the place. Piles of papers leaned drunkenly on the edge of the desk, looking as if they could topple over at any moment, and documents of every kind covered the floor.

What was the meaning of it? Had Mr Kendrick been the subject of a common burglary, or had one of his victims decided to reclaim their possessions without meeting his greedy demands?

She gave a sudden start as she heard a dull thud, then laughed with relief as she realized that it had been caused by nothing more than one of the piles of papers overbalancing and falling to the floor.

She turned her attention back to the papers. Could Arabella's letters be amongst them? she wondered. It was certainly possible. She was just about to start looking for them when she heard a sound from below. She felt her heart skip a beat. It was the sound of voices. And they were coming up the stairs.

Instinctively she backed away from the door . . . and found herself stopped by something large and hard. She gasped. And then her heart began to hammer in her chest. Whatever she had bumped into, it was not a piece of furniture. It was hard, but it had yielded a little as she had bumped into it, and it was warm.

Summoning her courage she told herself she must turn round, but before she could accomplish the act a hand reached round and clamped itself over her mouth and she was dragged forcibly backwards into a large cupboard, with her unknown assailant's arms wrapped tightly round her. Feeling an overwhelming need to get away, she bit into the fingers clamped over her mouth.

There was a stifled curse, and then a voice she recognized hissed in her ear, 'Don't fight me, you little fool. Keep still.'

'Lord Silverton!'

He pulled the cupboard door closed, and Eleanor felt her heart start to pound as she realized she was trapped in a confined space with the one man in all the world she did not want to be forced into close contact with. She could feel the hardness of his body at her back, and the ridged muscles of his arms and chest. His legs, long and lean, were pressed against hers and the feel of so much masculine strength made her tremble.

She did not know what danger awaited her outside the door but she began to feel it could not be any worse than this. She tried to move. If she could just inch forward she would not have to feel his body pressing so tightly against her. She pulled against his restraining arms and moved one leg, but this was even worse. The friction sent an unwelcome tremor coursing through her.

'Don't move,' he commanded.

She was about to make another effort to free herself, despite his warning, when she heard the voices drawing closer. They were now on the landing. She felt Lord Silverton tense again, and her own muscles tightened, too. She did not know what she had stumbled into, but it was obviously dangerous. She stopped struggling. For the first time she was glad of Lord Silverton's strength at her back.

Through a crack in the door she could see one of the men entering the room. He was tall and fair, and he was dressed in a brown tailcoat and breeches. She watched as he glanced around the room. 'It doesn't look as though there's anyone here.'

'Then what was that noise?' said the second

man.

'I don't know.'

The fair man looked round the room again and then, to her horror, she saw that his eyes had fallen on the cupboard. She forgot to breathe. He started to walk towards it . . . and then another of the piles of papers on the desk suddenly shifted under its own weight, before sliding with a soft *thump* on to the floor.

The man, his attention caught, cast his eye over the paper littering the floor, and seemed satisfied that the noise he had heard from downstairs had been caused by a similar slide. 'It was nothing,' he said. 'Just some papers shifting. Let's do what we came to do, then we can get out of here.'

The two men rifled the papers.

'Here they are,' said one of the men.

'Good. Let's go.'

Their steps could be heard going along the landing.

Eleanor began to breathe more normally again, but Lord Silverton's arms were still around her, and she knew she would have no peace until she had removed herself from his embrace. She made a move to pull away from him, but he held her firm.

'Wait,' he commanded.

She listened to the footsteps as they went down the stairs, and eventually she heard a soft *thunk* as the front door closed.

As soon as it had done so she struggled to

break free of his grasp. She needed to get out of the cupboard. Being so close to him made her feel vulnerable, and she had to escape. To her relief he let her go. Turning the handle she leant heavily against the cupboard door, and, in her haste she almost fell. Stumbling, she righted herself and quickly straightened up, resettling her bonnet and arranging the folds of her cloak in an effort to still her trembling nerves.

Lord Silverton followed her. She turned to face him, intending to berate him for dragging her into the cupboard, when she saw the look on his face and faltered. He wasn't smiling, as she had expected he would be, or throwing her a mocking glance. Instead he was glowering down at her, and his steely blue eyes were smouldering with unsuppressed anger.

'Now,' he said, 'suppose you tell me what the devil you are doing here?'

She took a step back and then stopped. She refused to be intimidated, even though he was looking dangerous enough to intimidate an entire army.

'I should have thought that was obvious,' she returned. 'I am trying to reclaim my letters.'

She saw his eyes narrow, as though trying to read her mind. His mouth suddenly hardened. 'Then you're a bloody little fool.'

Her eyes opened wide in astonishment. 'I beg your pardon?'

'Oh, no, you don't. You're far too pig-headed to do that.'

'Have you finished insulting me?' she asked, as anger took over from astonishment.

'I haven't even begun. You seek out Kendrick, knowing just what kind of man he is, and then you refuse to abandon your mission even when anyone but a fool would realize they were in over their head.'

'That's the second time you've called me a fool—'

'And it isn't enough? What the hell do you think you're doing, coming here and putting yourself in danger, and all to reclaim the letters of someone you don't even love?'

'Of course I love him,' she returned, taking exception to his high-handed attitude and determinedly protecting her sister by continuing the pretence that the compromising letters were her own. 'You know nothing about it.'

'I know you don't love him.'

'And how, pray, would you know that?' she demanded.

'Because of the way you react to me.'

She felt herself flush. There was a directness in his gaze that made her distinctly uncomfortable.

'I don't know what you're talking about,' she returned. But instead of sounding defiant her words came out half-heartedly, because she knew full well what he meant.

92

'Don't you?' he enquired. 'Then let me explain. When I kissed you, you kissed me back. And you did so passionately. Something you would not have done if you had been in love with another man.'

His eyes were boring into her own, and she was uncomfortably aware of the fact that she could not deny it.

Gathering the shreds of her dignity, she said, 'You will kindly remember who I am. And I would be obliged if you would not attempt to take any further liberties with my person,' she added as he took a step towards her and instinctively she took a step back.

'Oh? So that's what I was doing,' he asked mockingly. 'I was taking liberties with your person. I must remember that the next time—'

'There won't be a next time,' she interrupted him.

'No?'

His sardonic glance unsettled her. It was bad enough that, against her will, her heart leapt at the thought there would be a next time. It was even worse that he seemed to know it.

'Lord Silverton, you forget yourself,' she said repressively.

'Do I?' His eyes looked down into her own, and he took her hands. 'But all I am doing is speaking the truth.'

'The truth?' she enquired, trying to ignore the heat that surged through her at his touch.

'Your version of it, perhaps.'

'Can you deny it?' he asked, as he stroked the backs of her hands. There was still a trace of mockery in his voice, but there was a huskiness as well that made it difficult for her to think. 'There is an electrical connection between us, Eleanor.'

Try as she might, she could not deny it. The sparks that had flown between them when he had kissed her had been too intense to be gainsaid. Nevertheless, she could not give in to the magnetism he was exuding. Injecting the most scathing note she could manage into her voice she said, 'That has nothing to do with love.'

'Oh?' His eyebrows rose. 'I see.' His voice became even more husky. 'So it's lust?'

'Exactly,' she said defiantly, before realizing what she had said. 'No,' she contradicted herself hastily, feeling her heart beginning to race.

'Then if you don't lust after me you won't feel anything when I do this,' he said caressingly.

He trailed his finger along her jaw line, and she felt as though he had drawn a flaming torch across her skin. She tried to keep her voice steady. 'Definitely not.'

'Or this?'

His finger stroked up towards her mouth, then traced along the line of her lips.

Oh, it was heavenly! But she must not let

him know it. With great difficulty she fought down the trembling that threatened to consume her. 'No.'

It did not end there. 'Or this?' he asked, as his hand grazed the side of her throat.

'No!' She stepped backwards out of harm's way. She could not let him touch her again. It was driving her to distraction.

By his expression he obviously knew it.

'Forgive me,' he said.

But there was no repentance or desire for forgiveness in his voice. Instead there was a note of triumph.

'Believe me, Eleanor, it is better to discover your real feelings now, whilst you still have a chance to do something about it, rather than when it is too late,' he said.

His eyes looked directly into her own, and there was a moment of deep connection, as though his soul was speaking to hers.

She knew that what he said was true. If she had really imagined herself to be in love with the writer of the letters—if she had, perhaps, intended to marry her correspondent—then his actions would have made her think again. But she did not imagine herself to be in love with anyone. The situation was far more complicated than that.

'I know what my real feelings are,' she said, recovering herself, and speaking with as much haughtiness as she could muster. 'My real feelings are that no gentleman would treat a lady in the way you have just treated me.'

His eyes flashed. 'But then, I have never claimed to be a gentleman.'

As if to prove it, he pulled her roughly into his arms, and then he plundered her mouth with his own.

She should protest; push him away; but she was powerless to do it, because it was the most wonderful feeling. His kiss awakened new feelings in her, taking her beyond physical sensation and into the realms of emotion. He was like no man she had ever known before. He was dangerous and dictatorial, but perversely he made her feel wonderful—warm and wanted and *alive*.

And then her thoughts dissolved as he deepened the kiss, sending shock waves through her entire body. She wanted it to last for ever. Her head was light and her knees were weak, but it was the most wonderful thing she had ever experienced. And yet she must stop him. She tried to pull away, but his arms closed more firmly about her and she did not have the will to resist. Not until he lifted his mouth away from hers did she have the strength to take a step back.

'You . . . should not have done that,' she said, swallowing. Thinking, *And I should not have let you.*

'Oh, but you're wrong. It's exactly what I should have done. Because it was the only way to convince you, once and for all, that what you feel for your correspondent isn't love. You couldn't kiss me like that if you were in love with another man—no matter how much you lust after me,' he added wickedly. Then his mood sobered. 'I might not be a gentleman, Eleanor, but you are undoubtedly a lady, and you would never allow a man to kiss you if you had given your heart elsewhere. Give it up. Forget him. Leave the letters. Go home. There are forces at work here that you don't understand.'

'I can't.' She could no longer pretend that she was in love with the writer of the letters, but she had to make Lord Silverton understand why it was so important for her to reclaim them. If she did not, he would try and prevent her from looking for them, and would most likely put her into a hackney carriage himself. Unfortunately, there was only one way to make him understand. She would have to tell the truth.

She looked up, lifting her chin as her eyes met his in a direct gaze. 'You're right when you say that I don't love the writer of the letters. But you see, the letters aren't mine.'

'Ah.' She saw the understanding dawn on his face. 'But if they are not yours, then . . . ?'

She gave a sigh. 'They are my sister's.'

He nodded. 'That explains it. And she has some urgent reason for retrieving them. She is to be married, perhaps?' he asked.

'Yes. If the letters come to light it will cause

both her and her fiancé a great deal of distress, and it might jeopardize her future.'

'Of course,' he said to himself, as though he had just realized something. 'Miss Grantham. I should have recognized the name at once, but my mind has been on other matters recently. Your sister is to marry Charles . . . Charles Ormston, the son of the Duke of Brinsdale. I remember now.'

Eleanor nodded.

'I understand,' he said. 'She has written some compromising letters?'

'Some childish letters,' Eleanor corrected him, 'written when she was no more than seventeen. But they include girlish protestations of devotion, and Charles's family are very particular about such things.'

'Indeed they are,' he remarked drily.

'Yes. So you see, I have no choice. I have to find the letters.' She turned her attention back to the papers that littered the room. 'I hope they're here, and that I can manage to find them before Mr Kendrick returns.' She hesitated. 'Will you be looking for your letters, as well?'

He looked surprised.

'It's no use pretending,' she said.

She felt she had worked out the mystery of his strange behaviour, and she was determined to confront him with it.

'I don't believe your story about holding up the coach for a wager. If Mr Kendrick was blackmailing my sister, I see no reason why he would not be blackmailing other people, and it strikes me that one of them must have been you.' She hesitated. 'I can understand why you didn't want to give in to him, and why you decided to get your letters back by other means, but even so, you should not have held up the coach.'

He met her gaze, and she felt a disturbing hint of danger emanating from him. It was slight, but nevertheless it was there.

'I am not accustomed to having someone tell me what I should and should not do,' he said warningly. Then his eyes lit with a surprisingly teasing light. 'But perhaps that is because I have never met anyone brave enough to do it!'

She smiled. She could well believe it! Then she sobered. 'Even so, you should not have done it. The clergyman and the stout matron who were travelling with me were in fear for their lives. *You* might have known they were not in any danger, but they did not.'

The teasing light left his eyes. She could tell he did not want to talk about it. But she did. Although she understood his reasons—or so she thought—she did not approve of his methods, and was not afraid to say so.

'There must have been another way. Could you not have simply paid Mr Kendrick's price? For a man of your means it would not have been impossible.'

'Unfortunately,' he said softly, 'Mr Kendrick declined to sell.'

'Ah. I see. He meant to discredit you,' she said thoughtfully, following her own line of reasoning. 'Or the lady. Or both. Was it revenge?'

'Let's just say, he had another buyer.'

Eleanor tried to digest this, but could not make sense of it. She had the disturbing feeling that she had not got to the bottom of the mystery, after all.

'Let it go,' he said softly. 'Too much intelligence can be a dangerous thing—'

'In a woman?' she asked provocatively.

'In anyone.'

There was a change in the atmosphere and she was suddenly apprehensive. There was such a darkness about him that she felt as though she had stumbled into a puddle, only to find that instead of being two inches deep, it was bottomless. And that she was falling . . .

'I'll search the room myself,' he said. 'I'll find your sister's letters, as well as what I'm looking for, and then I'm putting you on the first stage heading back to Bath.'

Eleanor felt her spirits sink. Once he put her on a coach she would never see him again. She did not know why that should matter to her, but it did.

'In the meantime,' he continued, 'I suggest you go into one of the front rooms and keep watch at the window, so that you can warn me if Mr Kendrick returns.'

She was about to argue when she realized that it made sense. Leaving Lord Silverton she went out of the study and crossed the landing, going into a large and well-proportioned apartment that was evidently used as a dining-room. It was a spacious room, and Venetian mirrors on the walls made it seem even larger than it was. It had a moulded ceiling and elaborate cornices, an inlaid dining-table surrounded by Hepplewhite chairs, and several damasked sofas. Mr Kendrick had spared no expense.

Going past the table she walked over to the window. It was flanked by two red-damasked settees. She rounded the settees . . . and suddenly came to a stop. For there, sprawled on the floor behind the one to the left, was Mr Kendrick. And by the look of it he was dead.

She froze.

And then slowly she began to come back to life.

Her instinct was to back away from him, and she took a few steps towards the door, but then she stopped. Although a knife was sticking out of his back, she could not be sure that his wound was fatal. He might just be unconscious. Despite her distaste, she knew she should make sure. She overcame her revulsion and knelt down beside him. She took his hand. It was cold and limp. She felt for a pulse. But even as she did so she knew it was futile.

She dropped his hand and went back into the study, where Lord Silverton was kneeling on the floor, surrounded by a sea of papers. He looked up as she entered the room.

'You've seen Kendrick?' he asked.

She nodded.

'Damn. And I was just getting started. I hoped I'd have longer. But if he is here then we will have to go.'

'No. You don't understand.'

He looked at her more closely, and then his eyes became concerned. 'You're as white as a sheet,' he said. 'What's happened?'

'It's Mr Kendrick,' she said, her voice shaking. 'I haven't seen him, I've found him. In the room across the corridor. He's dead.'

'Dead?' he demanded.

She nodded mutely.

He dropped the papers he was holding and went over to her, taking her hands between his.

'You're freezing,' he said, chafing them.

'I'm all right,' she protested.

'No. You're not. And it isn't surprising. You've had a shock. But I must go and make certain for myself that Kendrick's really dead. Wait here.'

Before she could protest he was out of the room, and a few minutes later he returned. He gave her a brief nod. 'You're right. He's been dead for some time.'

He swept up the papers he had not yet had time to look through and looked round for something to put them in. A portmanteau was stored behind the desk. He put the papers inside, then closed the catch.

'Come,' he said. 'It's time for us to leave.'

'Shouldn't we inform the authorities?'

'We will. Or rather, I will. But right now I want to get you home.'

She shook her head. The last thing she wanted to do was to get on a stagecoach. 'I don't think I can face it,' she said. A reaction to events was setting in, and she felt suddenly weak. 'The journey—if I could have something to eat first . . .'

He took her chin between his fingers and an unmistakable look of tenderness lit his eyes. 'I was not suggesting you should travel back to Bath. You're not going to your home. You're going to mine.'

CHAPTER FIVE

Her eyes widened in surprise. And then she shook her head. 'I can't go with you to your home.'

'There is no suitable coach until the morning, and I'm not letting you out of my sight until you're on it,' he returned.

'But I can't spend the night beneath your

roof.'

'Whoever murdered Kendrick might not be far away, and if they suspect you know something you will be in danger,' he said. 'But you will be safe with me.'

Reluctantly Eleanor nodded. Dangerous though Lord Silverton was, she knew he would protect her. He was used to dealing with perilous situations, and she was not. Besides, she was still suffering from the shock of finding Mr Kendrick's body and she welcomed the chance to rest for a while in safety. However, there was one last thing that worried her. 'If anyone sees me—'

'We will not go together, and as long as you make sure the street is empty before going inside then no one will know you are there.' He gave her directions of how to get to Silverton House. 'It's less than a five-minute walk away,' he finished. 'When my valet, Beddows, opens the door—the rest of the servants have not yet returned from my country estate, as my town house has been shut up over the summer—give him this.' He took a signet ring from his finger. 'He is a very discreet individual, and will let you in without asking any questions.'

Eleanor hesitated. She could not help wondering how many other women had presented the ring to Lord Silverton's 'very discreet' valet in order to be admitted without any questions being asked.

'And no,' he said, reading her expression correctly and giving her a wolfish smile, 'I don't make a habit of this.'

'I never said you did,' she returned, flustered.

'But you thought it.'

The smile that went with his words was disarming, and despite herself she smiled in return.

'Lord Silverton, too much intelligence is a dangerous thing,' she said, using his own words against him.

'In a man?' he asked.

She laughed.

He laughed, too. *'Touché!'* he said.

He took her hand between his strong fingers. Then holding it up in front of him he slid the ring on to her finger.

There seemed something intimate about the gesture. Her eyes flew to his, and she could tell from his expression that the same thought had struck him, too. Their gazes held.

Then he dropped her hand.

Standing back to let her go through the door, he said, 'Go as quickly as you can but don't run and don't look round. I will be right behind you.'

She went down the stairs and out into the street.

The day had become wet. Persistent rain fell from the louring sky, and few people were braving the elements. Before many minutes had passed Eleanor had reached Silverton House and was knocking on the door.

Controlling her impatience, she waited for an answer to her summons. It came quickly. She lifted her hand, but before she had a chance to speak, Beddows noticed the ring on her finger and opened the door wide to let her in.

'Your master is following close behind,' she said.

He nodded wordlessly and closed the door.

She had just time to undo the strings of her bonnet before the door opened again and Lord Silverton let himself in.

'Well done,' he said. 'I don't believe we were noticed.' He smiled. 'Welcome to my home.'

Eleanor felt a stirring of curiosity and found herself looking forward to seeing where he lived.

Beddows took her cloak and bonnet, and then Lord Silverton led her into a small parlour at the back of the house. It was a cheerful room, with a bright fire blazing in the hearth. The furniture was somewhat battered but it was homely, and obviously well loved. A sofa was pushed back against the wall, its warm colours glowing in the firelight. There was a small table next to it. A couple of armchairs, one with the stuffing peeping out, flanked the fire, whilst a colourful rug lay in front of it.

So there is warmth to his personality as well

as hardness, she thought.

She had seen flashes of it over the last twenty-four hours, but little more. Up until now, she had seen him only in dangerous or tense situations, but here she was seeing him in the relaxed environment of his home. Already it had changed him. He seemed more approachable. His face had lost some of its hard lines and planes. The masculine contours had softened, making him seem younger and more good-humoured. The thought made her blossom inside. It seemed the evening might be an enjoyable one after all.

A brief twinge assailed her as she thought of the impropriety but she dismissed it. She was not a young girl, to be afraid of the company of a man. Nor did she feel herself to be in danger. Despite the fact that Lord Silverton had kissed her she did not feel intimidated by him, and knew that she could have stopped him at any time, if she had wanted to. To her shame, she knew that she had not.

It was something she did not care to think about. It led her thoughts down too many new and unsettling paths that she did not wish to explore. Such as, why did she burn at his touch? Why did she allow her feelings to overcome her good sense when he was near? Why could she not bear the thought of returning to Bath? And why did she feel hollow at the thought of never seeing him again?

Determinedly putting all such thoughts out of her mind, she looked around the room. Her eyes came to rest on a number of curious fixtures attached to the walls.

He followed her gaze.

'Gas lighting,' he said.

He lit a taper from the fire and then, turning on the gas, he lit it. A pure and brilliant light was cast over the room.

'Goodness,' said Eleanor, startled by its brightness. 'I had no idea it was so powerful.' She turned to him with interest. 'Had you seen it working before you decided to have it installed?'

'It wasn't my idea.'

He motioned her to sit down and she took one of the chairs by the fire. He seemed to be in a mood to talk, and she was interested to learn more about his life.

He took the chair opposite her and stretched out his long legs in front of him, crossing one booted ankle over the other.

'My father was always interested in new inventions and he was convinced that gas was the future,' he explained. 'He saw an article about it in *Ackermann's Repository* last year and he had it installed in Silverton House.'

'I remember seeing the article,' said Eleanor, who took the popular journal. It was one of the few small luxuries she and Arabella allowed themselves, and they enjoyed reading the articles on modern life as well as looking at the delectable fashion plates. 'But I thought most people were still convinced that gas is only fit for factories?'

'There are still one or two problems to overcome,' he admitted. 'The amount of heat it gives out will need to be looked at, and there is a noticeable smell, but I still think my father was right. The light is so much brighter than candles that one day I'm convinced it will be in every home.'

Eleanor's eyes drifted to a portrait hanging next to the door.

'Is that your father?' she asked.

He nodded. 'That is the last portrait I have of him. It was painted shortly before his death.'

His death must have been quite recent, Eleanor realized, as he had installed the gas-lighting only the previous year. Her sympathy was aroused. Lord Silverton was a strong man, and yet it was evident from his expression and tone of voice that he had loved his father. He was capable of deep feelings. The thought made her feel strangely vulnerable. If ever he were to fall in love, the woman he fell in love with would experience the full depth of those feelings. It would be no superficial experience, but one that was profound and meaningful.

Fortunately for her peace of mind the door opened at that moment, and Beddows entered the room. The valet was obviously used to turning his hand to a variety of things, as he was carrying a tea tray. Eleanor looked gratefully at the silver teapot. Although she had recovered from the shock of finding Mr Kendrick's body, it had been an unpleasant incident and it had left her feeling drained. She welcomed a hot drink.

'Thank you, Beddows,' said Lord Silverton.

'My lord.' Beddows bowed his way out of the room.

Lord Silverton poured her a cup of tea and handed it to her. 'Here, drink this,' he said. 'You'll soon feel better.'

'You shouldn't be waiting on me,' she said uncomfortably.

He raised one eyebrow. 'Oh? Why not?'

'Because you're an earl.'

'I'm also a gentleman—at least by birth,' he added with a twinkle in his eye, '—and a gentleman always waits on a lady.'

She smiled. He was teasing her again!

She took a sip of tea. It was sweet and hot. 'Ah!' She felt her strength begin to return.

With her renewed vigour, however, came the recollection that so far they had done nothing about reporting the death of Mr Kendrick.

'Lord Silverton—' she began.

'Lucien,' he interrupted her.

She looked up, startled.

'My name is Lucien.'

His voice had softened, and he was looking at her in a disturbingly gentle way.

'I don't think . . .' she began.

'That you should call me by my name?'

'No.' She turned her cup between her hands.

He had called her by her name several times at Mr Kendrick's house, and at the time she had not felt equal to remonstrating with him. But now she was capable of doing so, and of resisting him when he asked her to call him by his given name.

'Why not?'

His eyes were on her, and she knew that he wanted a genuine answer. He was intrigued as to what she thought, and he wanted to know what she had to say.

She put down her cup. 'Because it is wrong.'

'Do you believe that?' he asked.

'I . . .' She had never thought about it. When she did so, she realized that although society believed it was wrong, she did not. But she did believe it was dangerous. Calling him Lucien removed a barrier between them, and just now she needed every barrier she could find. She had been opening up to the warmth of his personality ever since she had set foot in the house, and she must do everything in her power to resist him.

'I think it would be better if I continued to call you Lord Silverton,' she said firmly.

'But I don't. Lord Silverton, to me, is still my father,' he explained. 'He died so recently that I don't feel I belong to that name. When I

111

am out in society's ballrooms, I have no choice, but here I like to be myself.'

Eleanor remembered the way Mrs Oliver had constantly used his title, and knew exactly what he meant. Matchmaking mamas liked nothing better than to call him 'My lord', as it reminded them of how eligible he was.

'I would prefer it if you called me Lucien,' he said.

The idea was growing more and more appealing. And no one would be able to take exception to it, as no one would hear her. Besides, it would be for one evening only, she thought. Tomorrow she would be on her way.

She nodded. 'Very well.'

He smiled. This time the smile was not wry, it was a smile of genuine warmth. There was a moment of connection between them. To hide from it, for she found it alarming, she turned the conversation into more practical channels. 'We must tell the authorities about Mr Kendrick,' she said.

'I have a . . . colleague . . . coming here this evening. In fact,' said Lucien, glancing at the ormòlu clock on the mantelpiece, 'he will be here shortly. He is reliable and discreet, and he will see to all the formalities.'

'You don't want to get involved,' said Eleanor, realizing this was so.

'No. I don't want to risk getting entangled with the authorities. And I want to make sure that you are not dragged in. Drayforth will take care of everything.'

Eleanor nodded. She did not want to be mixed up in a murder investigation, particularly not now with Arabella's wedding fast approaching. There was no point in her rescuing her sister from one potential scandal, only to plunge her into another.

'Do you think the two men we saw were responsible for Mr Kendrick's death?' she asked.

He was thoughtful.

'It's possible. Or they might have been there on some other errand, simply retrieving letters of their own.'

They fell silent.

As she sat sipping her tea, Eleanor felt Lord Silverton's eyes wandering over her face. He was like no other man she had met before. He was strong and powerful, with an edge of danger, and yet there was evidently much more to him than that. Not only did he have a sense of humour that she had not suspected, he had a desire to protect her. It was something she had not known before. Her father had died when she had been young, and her mother had been an invalid, so that it had been up to Eleanor to manage the household. Her mother and Arabella had leant on her, and she had never minded, because by virtue of her health and her age she was the member of the family most able to carry the burdens of life. But it warmed her through to know that here was someone who cared about her enough to protect her from unpleasantness. It made her feel stronger, somehow. More open. Because she knew that if she stumbled he would be there to catch her.

At least until she returned to Bath.

Her thoughts were disturbed by a knock at the outside door. Lucien put down his cup.

'That will be Drayforth,' he said. 'I shouldn't be long. He will not stay for more than half an hour, and then after that we will have dinner.'

He left the room.

Eleanor continued to sip her tea by the fire.

When she had finished, her gaze strayed to the portmanteau which Lucien had left by the table. Whilst he was busy with his guest, she decided to look for Arabella's letters.

She pulled the portmanteau out into the middle of the room and emptied it in front of her, then set about sorting through the large pile of papers. As she did so she wondered whether she would come across Lucien's letters. If, indeed, he had been in search of love letters.

When she had seen him at Mr Kendrick's house she had been certain of it. It had seemed to explain his strange behaviour when they had first met, as well as his presence at Mr Kendrick's house, but now she was not so sure. However, it was still a possibility, and she felt reluctant to find them. It would be the height of bad manners for her to catch a glimpse of their contents, she told herself. But she could not disguise from herself that her reasons went deeper than that. In some way she did not fully understand she did not want to see them because they would hurt her.

But Arabella's letters had to be found.

She continued sorting through the letters until a faint scent caught her nostrils. She recognized the perfume: lavender. It was one her mother had worn, and one Arabella had often borrowed. It was very faint, but unmistakable.

She followed her nose, and found a small bundle of letters tied together with a pink ribbon. She pulled the bow and unfastened the letters. Yes! They were Arabella's. Her task was done.

She gave a sigh of relief. Now that the letters had been found, Arabella's future happiness was safe.

As she sat back on her heels, her own problem solved, she wondered what to do with all the other love letters. It seemed dreadful that innocent people—innocent, at least, of any crime—should continue to pay because they believed themselves to be in danger of exposure, but that's just what they would have to do if the letters fell into the wrong hands.

Could she return them to their rightful owners? she wondered. And if so, how should she do it? A direct approach would be fraught with difficulties. Quite apart from having to visit the people concerned, there would be the possibility that they might take her for an accomplice.

She resolved to ask Lucien for his opinion when he returned.

In the meantime she set Arabella's letters on the table and started putting the other papers back in the portmanteau. As she did so, an unusual document caught her eye. It was on heavy paper, and was written in a clear hand. Troop deployments, supply lines . . . With a shock she realized that she was looking at secret military information. And then realization dawned. That was why Lucien had held up the stage. He had done it in order to retrieve stolen military documents. The more she thought about it, the more it made sense. He had been in the army, Mrs Oliver had said. And evidently, although he had sold his commission on inheriting the title, he was still helping the war effort. Only this time, in more covert ways.

She was certain she had at last found the answer to the mystery. It was far more likely that he would hold up a stagecoach for the good of the country than for some minor private affair—although she was still puzzled as to why it had been necessary. It seemed easier, on the face of it, for him to have simply arrested Mr Kendrick instead of carrying out a charade. But she knew Lucien well enough to be certain there must have been a good reason for his actions, even if she did not yet know what it was.

She was relieved. Instead of being a wastrel who had engaged in a petty wager, he was a man she could respect. But the realization, instead of warming her, unsettled her, because it made him even more appealing. And even more difficult to resist. She had never had any difficulty in resisting masculine charms before. The gentlemen she had met in Bath, together with those she had met whilst chaperoning Arabella for her London Season, had been pleasant enough, but they had been inconsequential. She had never felt a need for them, or had more than a superficial desire to be in their company. She had enjoyed talking to them and dancing with them, but they had never been important to her happiness. And now here was Lucien, showing her that life had more to offer than she had ever expected. That he was a man she *wanted* to be with.

It shook her to realize how much she wanted to be with him. He made her feel more vital, more fulfilled, more alive than she had ever felt before.

But in the morning she would leave London, and she would never see him again.

Her heart sank. She could not bear to think of it.

To distract her thoughts, she began to put the rest of the documents back in the portmanteau, but her movements were mechanical, and no matter how much she tried to dismiss Lucien from her mind she found it was impossible.

*   *   *

'Well?' Drayforth was sitting back against the desk in the library. 'Did you retrieve the documents?'

He was a stocky man, small compared to Lucien, although still of medium height. He had intelligent eyes, a firm mouth and a decided chin. His clothes were well-tailored and his boots were highly polished. He could easily pass for a man about town. But he was much more than that. Like Lucien, he was involved in the Kendrick affair.

Lucien nodded. 'Yes.'

'Ah.' Drayforth let out a sigh of relief.

'Drink?' asked Lucien. He was standing by a small table on which stood a selection of bottles, holding a decanter.

'No, not for me,' said Drayforth easily. 'But you go ahead.'

'No, not for me either,' said Lucien, restoppering the decanter. 'I'd rather keep a clear head.'

Drayforth nodded. 'Save it for after dinner!' he said.

Lucien sat down in a wing chair and crossed one booted foot over the other.

'So the hold-up went as planned?' asked Drayforth, sitting down opposite Lucien.

Lucien frowned. 'No. In fact, quite the opposite. I held up the stagecoach as arranged, but Kendrick didn't have the documents on him.'

'No?'

'No.'

'But our information was definite,' declared Drayforth. 'Our intelligence clearly told us that he would be transporting the documents to London in a case.'

'I know. Which means that either our intelligence was wrong—it does happen—or Kendrick changed his mind.'

Drayforth regarded Lucien enquiringly. 'Then if he didn't have them in his case, how . . . ?'

'I followed Kendrick to London, and broke into his house in Pall Mall.'

Drayforth pursed his lips. 'Risky,' he said, shaking his head.

'Perhaps. But it had to be done. I was out of options.'

Reluctantly, Drayforth nodded. 'I suppose so. Still, as long as you got hold of them in the end, that's the main thing. You weren't discovered, I take it? Kendrick didn't see you?'

Lucien looked moodily ahead of him. 'There has been a complication.'

Drayforth waited.

'Kendrick is dead.'

'*What?*' Drayforth started up.

Briefly, Lucien told Drayforth of what had happened that afternoon.

Drayforth let out a low whistle, and reseated himself. 'So someone got to Kendrick.' He became thoughtful. 'Do you have any idea who it was?'

Lucien shook his head. 'No. He was mixed up in all sorts of unsavoury enterprises— blackmail, to name but one—as well as stealing and selling military secrets. He must have had a lot of enemies.'

'So you think his death had nothing to do with his treachery?'

'It might have done. But then again, it might not. It seems to me that any number of people might have wanted to see him dead.'

'It's a pity. We could have used him. Still, it can't be helped. If he's dead, he's dead.'

'I haven't yet notified the authorities—'

'You can leave that to me.'

'I was hoping you'd say that. I don't want to get involved.'

'Quite right too. You'd get bogged down with the investigation, and awkward questions might be asked. It's much better for all concerned if you stay out of it. It will save you the trouble of answering questions, and besides, we don't want anyone to guess at your involvement with the government. As far as the world knows, you left the army when you inherited your title and you've had nothing to do with either the army or the government since. That suits us. It means we can use you whenever necessary for a dangerous mission without anyone suspecting you might be involved.'

Lucien nodded. 'That leaves the problem of Kendrick. What will you do, have someone "find" the body?'

'Yes. We'll make sure it's someone of unimpeachable character, who also has a good reason for being there. They can claim to have had an appointment with Kendrick and then they can answer all the necessary questions. That way the matter will be dealt with quickly and efficiently.' He paused. 'Did you find anything else at Kendrick's?' he asked.

'I've brought away a portmanteau full of papers. If I discover anything else of importance I'll pass it on to the general.'

'Good. With any luck we'll get even more than we bargained for. Do you want me to take the documents now? I'll be seeing the general later on tonight.'

'No.' Lucien shook his head. 'I want to speak to him myself. I'll be seeing him first thing in the morning, and I'll give him the documents then. They'll still be in time to be of use.'

Drayforth stood up. 'Very well. I won't keep you. I have things to do, and so have you.'

Lucien stood up, too. 'Until the next time.'

'Yes. We'll probably be working together

121

again soon. Let's hope all our ventures are as successful as this one.'

'Agreed.'

Lucien rang the bell for Beddows.

'Don't worry,' said Drayforth. 'I'll show myself out.'

Lucien, a smile crossing his face as he thought of Eleanor, was only too happy to let him.

*   *   *

Eleanor was putting away the last of the papers when she heard the door begin to open. She felt her spirits sink. Lucien had said he would look for her sister's letters himself, and now she understood why. It was because he had not wanted her to find the military documents. How would he react now that she had done so? she wondered apprehensively.

Although a rapport had started to build between them over the last few hours, this was a dangerous situation and she had no idea what he might do or say.

She watched his face carefully when he walked into the room, ready for whatever situation should arise.

He looked surprised to begin with, when he saw her kneeling on the floor instead of sitting in a chair as he had left her, but then his eyes drifted to the portmanteau and his face became dark.

122

'What the devil do you think you're doing?' he demanded, his voice hard.

Eleanor felt her throat go dry. There was no point in prevaricating. If a storm was about to break it might as well do so at once.

'Looking for my sister's letters,' she returned. 'Fortunately, I have found them.'

His eyes held hers. 'And a lot more besides.'

There was no use denying it. 'Yes.'

There was a long silence.

At last he said, 'So now you know why I held up the stage.'

'I do. To retrieve the documents.'

As he hadn't exploded, she thought perhaps they would be able to have a conversation about the matter.

'But what I still don't understand is why you couldn't simply have arrested Mr Kendrick if you knew he was a traitor. It would have made a lot more sense than frightening innocent people.'

'That was regrettable. But unavoidable. Even so, don't forget, a speedy end to the war will be good for everyone, including the people on the stagecoach.'

Eleanor remembered the conversation that had followed the hold-up, how the stout matron had declared that her son was in the army, and how the clergyman had added that his nephew was also on the Continent. They might have been frightened at the time, but she had a feeling that if they had known what

123

Lucien was really doing, they would not have objected to his masquerade.

'But I still don't see why it was necessary,' she said.

'Then I will explain.'

He sat down, stretching his long legs out in front of him.

'When we discovered that Kendrick was stealing secret military documents and selling them to the French we had a number of options open to us. We could have arrested him for being a traitor, but if we had done so we would have missed an opportunity.' His eyes snapped to hers. 'How much do you know about the war?'

'Very little,' she confessed. 'I don't take a newspaper, and as I don't know anyone in the army or the navy I hear little about it.'

Lucien's mood darkened. 'The war is not going well. After some early victories we have suffered a number of recent defeats. If we don't stop Napoleon soon, we may not be able to stop him at all. We need an edge. And Kendrick's treachery gave us one. We knew that if we could retrieve the stolen documents without him knowing that we had discovered his perfidy, then we could leave other documents in his way. Only this time, they would contain false information. That way, when he stole them and sold them on, he would be unwittingly misleading the enemy.'

'I see.' She was pleased that he had

explained it to her. But then an unwelcome side to the situation occurred to her. Now that he had told her such secrets, what would he do with her?

He looked at her enquiringly.

'You have told me a great deal of sensitive information,' she said hesitantly.

'Ah. I see. You think I might be going to keep you under lock and key?'

She thought exactly that. But whether he was teasing her by his words, or whether he was being deadly serious she could not tell.

'It would be one way of keeping you out of trouble,' he remarked. But this time, there was an unmistakable note of humour in his voice.

Her mouth quirked.

His own quirked in answer. Then he became serious. 'You have kept my secret this far, Eleanor. I believe I can trust you, now you know the whole.'

His belief in her made her feel warm inside.

At that moment Beddows entered the room.

'Dinner is served, my lord.'

'Good.' Lucien stood up and offered Eleanor his arm.

After a moment's hesitation she took it. The feel of his muscles beneath his tailcoat was stimulating.

To distract her thoughts from their wayward channels, she said, 'What will you do with the letters? They should be returned to their owners, but I don't see how it's to be done.'

'Beddows will see to it,' said Lucien, as they went through the hall. 'He knows the servants in almost every London house of importance, and he can arrange for the letters to be returned discreetly.'

'Good. I don't like to think of people living in fear, worrying that their secrets are going to be revealed. Nor do I like the thought of someone else finding the letters and using them to blackmail people again.'

'Blackmail's an ugly business,' he agreed.

They went into the dining-room. Like the small sitting-room, it was evidently a room to be used and enjoyed. The wallpaper was old-fashioned and the green silk curtains were faded. The carved mantelpiece had a chip out of the bottom of it, and the scuff marks on the mahogany table showed that the room had been loved, lived in and well used.

'A particularly lively tussle with the family dog,' he said, laughing, as he saw her looking at a large scratch on one of the table legs. 'I will never forget my mother's horror as Prince's claws scraped down the table.' His eyes twinkled. 'Needless to say, my brothers and I were in disgrace. We were not meant to play with the dog in here. As a punishment we had to eat in the nursery for a week!'

'And the dog?' enquired Eleanor humorously.

'He was banned from the dining-room altogether. Although he managed to sneak in

126

now and again when no one was looking!'

Eleanor laughed at this glimpse into his childhood.

He pulled out one of the chairs for her, and she sat down.

'I don't usually bother with a fire in here,' he said, glancing towards the empty grate, 'but if you are not warm enough, Beddows can light one.'

'That isn't necessary,' she said.

She could see why he would not normally have a fire in this room. It faced south, and it was warmed by the sun streaming in at the tall windows. Even now, in the early evening, the room was pleasantly warm. He seated himself at the other end of the table.

'How many brothers do you have?' she asked, interested to know more of his family.

'I had two.' His mood became darker. 'My elder brother, Henry, died when I was on the Continent.'

'I'm sorry,' she said.

'So am I. He died of cholera. My mother died in the same outbreak. He would have made an excellent earl. He loved all the pomp and circumstance, but he was a natural landowner, too. He was interested in innovations, like my father, and wanted to introduce new farming methods to make our estates even more profitable. And he wanted the tenants to take a share. He wanted their fortunes to be bound up with our own, so that

127

if the estate prospered, then so did they.'

'He was forward thinking,' remarked Eleanor.

'He was. It was a great tragedy for the family, and also for the estate when he died. I will do my best for the estate now that I have inherited, but I am not a farmer.'

'Your abilities lie in other directions.'

Beddows entered the room, putting a plate of mutton broth in front of each of them.

'I live simply when I'm here on my own,' said Lucien by way of explanation.

'You said you had two brothers?' asked Eleanor as Beddows left the room.

'Yes. I have a younger brother, too. His name is Edwin. He's at Eton, and looks likely to be a scholar.'

Over dinner the conversation flowed. Eleanor found it surprising how easy it was to talk to him. Now that they were removed from difficult and dangerous situations, and now that she understood his motives in holding up the stagecoach, she was discovering they shared a strong rapport. She enjoyed his company. He was a man of many facets, and the more she saw, the more she felt drawn to him, and she found herself telling him far more than she had intended to. She told him about Arabella, about her parents and about her early life. He understood her readily, and she was surprised to find how quickly the meal had gone when Beddows brought in the drinks' tray. If there had been other guests, she would have retired with the ladies, leaving the gentlemen to their port. But as it was, there was no point in her withdrawing alone, and she felt it was time for her to say goodnight.

Lucien did not try to detain her.

'Beddows has prepared a room for you,' he said. 'He will show you the way. Then first thing tomorrow I will put you on the stagecoach and send you home.'

Eleanor's spirits fell. Tomorrow would be the last time she would see Lucien. She was bitterly disappointed. She had known him for such a short space of time that she should not have any feelings for him. Yet she had.

'I can rely on you to forget that you ever heard the name Kendrick?' he asked her, as he stood looking down at her.

'Of course.' She spoke evenly, so that he would not guess how painful it was for her to be parting from him.

'Good. Even dead, he is not a good man to talk about. Your sister, too, should forget she ever heard the name.'

'I understand.'

He looked at her for long moments, and then he opened the door and Beddows showed her to her room.

*   *   *

The clock chimed eleven, and then half past.

Eleanor was in bed, but she could not sleep. The day had been full of so many disturbing incidents, and the evening full of so many unexpected pleasures that she found she could not rest. Her mind kept turning over the events of the day, culminating in the final event when Beddows had showed her to her room, a pretty chamber with a four-poster bed and a comfortable chair by the fire. It had sprigged drapes at the windows, and a sprigged coverlet over the bed, and like the rest of the house, it had a lived-in air.

It had been delightful to wash in the hot water Beddows had left in her room after stripping off her travel-stained clothing and then slipping between the sheets. But to her dismay she had not been able to sleep. And now she at last gave into wakefulness and sat up in bed.

Perhaps she could find something to read. That usually helped.

She threw back the covers and climbed out of bed. A glimmer of moonlight shone through a crack in the curtains, enabling her to see. She looked around for something to read, but there were no books, and not even a journal was to be found.

She recalled that Lucien had seen Drayforth in the library that evening. Then the house certainly had one. What sort of books did it contain? she wondered. There was only one way to find out. She slipped on her pelisse and made her way downstairs.

The house was silent. She went along the landing and down the stairs, moving cautiously so that she did not tread on a squeaking floorboard and waken Lucien or Beddows. Then she went through the hall. As she approached the dining-room, however, her steps began to falter. There was something foul in the air. She stopped, and then went on again. What could it be? She did not know. But with each step she found it more and more difficult to breathe.

And then she recognized the smell. Gas!

Lucien had mentioned its smell earlier in the evening, and she had noticed it particularly. But now it was much stronger. It seemed that the new-fangled lighting must have sprung a leak.

She covered her face with her hand and turned away, intending to rouse the house, when a glance through the open door of the dining-room showed her a leg. With a sickening thud in her chest she realized that someone was in the room . . . and from the length of the leg, there was only one person it could be.

Lucien!

All thoughts of rousing the house dissolved in the presence of this new calamity. Lucien was in there! Her heart began to beat more quickly. She had to get him out.

Lifting her pelisse and holding it in front of

her face to protect her as much as possible from the evil gas, she made a determined run into the room. Her worst fears were realized. Lucien was slouched in a wing chair, and from the look of it he was unconscious.

How long had he been under the influence of the gas? she asked herself.

She did not know. Nor did she have time to wonder. She seized the jug of water that stood on the drinks tray and dashed it in his face in an attempt to bring him round.

He did not stir.

She took him by the shoulders and tried to shake him into consciousness, but again to no avail.

In desperation she took him by the arm and tried to pull him towards the door. At first she thought it was going to be impossible, but at last she managed to slide him out of the chair and across the floor. It was difficult work. He was a large man, and a heavy one. But panic gave her strength, and at last she managed to pull him out of the room. She dropped his arm and closed the door, shutting as much of the evil air inside as possible.

What to do next? She should rouse him, but she didn't know how.

Beddows would know. Beddows, with his wide-ranging experience. Her eyes flew upwards, wondering in what room Beddows was sleeping. She must find it quickly and wake him. And then a simpler answer came to her as her eyes fell on the dinner gong.

Dropping Lucien's arm, she went over to the gong and gave it a resounding strike. The noise reverberated through the house. In little more than a minute, it brought Beddows running on to the landing in his nightshirt.

'What the . . . ?' he demanded, looking down into the hall.

'It's Lucien,' said Eleanor urgently. 'He was in the dining-room. The gas was leaking. He's unconscious.'

Beddows quickly became matter of fact. Running down the stairs he joined Eleanor in the hall, and looked at his supine master.

'A gas leak, you say?' he demanded.

Eleanor nodded.

Swiftly taking in the situation, Beddows lifted one of Lucien's arms and instructed Eleanor to lift the other, and together they half-carried, half-dragged him into the library. It was far enough away from the dining-room to have escaped the taint, and it provided them with a place in which to revive him. Setting him down on *a chaise-longue*, they pushed him back into a reclining position.

'The gas . . .' said Eleanor, glancing towards the door.

Beddows understood her immediately and went out of the room, leaving her alone with Lucien.

Now that the immediate danger was past she found that she was trembling. To see

Lucien like this, when he was usually so vital, shocked her to the core. His skin looked unhealthy and his chest was rising and falling in uneven bursts. She felt the cold grip of fear. If anything should happen to him . . . It was now useless to tell herself that he meant nothing to her, that she had known him for so short a time that she could not possibly have feelings for him. Because she did. She had profound feelings for him that went beyond the rational and tapped into the depths of her being.

She felt so helpless. She could do little for him, but what she could do, she did. She arranged his body in a more comfortable attitude across the *chaise longue* and then brought a chair for his feet. Next she brought a cushion and put it beneath his head. His skin was looking slightly healthier, and she felt hope stirring. Perhaps he had not been under the influence of the gas for very long.

She loosened his cravat so that he could breathe more easily, and pushed back a lock of hair that had fallen across his brow, then sat down by his side to watch over him.

It seemed a long time before Beddows returned, and in all that time she saw very little change in Lucien. It was an anxious vigil. But by and by there came small improvements. His breathing became easier, his colour returned, and his eyelids flickered. He stirred slightly, and shifted his position.

'How is he?' asked Beddows, coming quietly into the room.

'He seems a little better. He stirred just now.'

Beddows joined her and looked down at Lucien.

'Yes. He looks a lot better. He'll be regaining consciousness soon.'

'Have you been able to stop the leak?' asked Eleanor. She did not want Beddows to know how affected she was by Lucien's predicament, and strove to keep the conversation matter of fact.

'There was no leak,' he said. 'The lights had blown out, so the gas was coming into the room without being burnt.'

'I wondered whether the lights were safe,' said Eleanor. She carried on the conversation with Beddows, but her eyes kept drifting to Lucien, no matter how hard she tried to keep them on his valet. 'Gas is such a new form of lighting there are bound to be problems with it. Candles might not give such a strong light, but at least they cannot cause this kind of harm.'

Beddows frowned. 'It's never happened before.'

'But it has now. Have you turned it off?'

Beddows, recalling himself to the present, reassured her, saying, 'Yes, I've turned it off and opened the windows. It should soon disperse.'

'Lu—Lord Silverton should have a doctor,' she said, looking at him once more.

'No.'

'No?'

'It will be for him to decide, once he comes round,' said Beddows.

Eleanor began to wonder whether there was more to the situation than met the eye. But at that moment Lucien stirred more vigorously, then he gave a cough and opened his eyes.

'Lie still,' said Eleanor, pushing him gently back on to the *chaise-longue* as he tried to get up.

'. . . Eleanor?' His voice was weak, and his eyes did not focus.

'Yes. I'm here.'

He closed his eyes, then opened them again. This time they focused on her. 'What am I doing on the *chaise*?'

He tried to sit up.

'You have had an accident,' she said. 'The lights blew out in the dining-room and you breathed in a lot of gas.'

He lay back, collapsing against the *chaise*, not yet strong enough to sit up. He lay quietly for a few minutes. Then, evidently gaining strength, he asked, 'Why am I in the library?'

'I found you unconscious, and dragged you in here to get you out of the foul air,' said Eleanor.

He smiled weakly. 'Eleanor, you surprise me more every day.'

136

His eyes looked into her own, and she trembled. They were softer than she had ever seen them. Their blue was an ever-changing shade, now steely, now as blue as the heavens. And their depths drew her in.

'It's lucky Miss Grantham found you when she did,' said Beddows. 'If she hadn't gone into the dining-room it could have been very nasty.'

Lucien looked at her enquiringly.

'I will explain everything later. But for now you must rest.'

'It will help me to do so if I know what happened,' he said.

She could see that he meant it. 'Very well. I couldn't sleep,' she said. 'I wanted to get a book from the library, so I came downstairs.'

'It's lucky for me you did.' He tried to sit up again, and this time he managed to do it. Even so, although his feet were now on the floor, he leaned back against the *chaise* when he had accomplished it. He directed an enquiring look at Beddows. 'I wonder why the burners blew out.'

'I don't know,' said Beddows blandly. 'But I'll make sure it doesn't happen again.'

Lucien nodded.

Eleanor was relieved to see that his colour had improved, and that his breathing had returned to normal. He was shaking off his grogginess, and was looking more alert with every passing minute. It had been an anxious time—she did not want to admit to herself just

137

how anxious—but to her relief she realized it had passed. He did not seem to have taken any permanent harm from the incident, and she was just grateful that she had not been able to sleep.

'Even so, I don't understand why you didn't notice the lights blowing out,' said Eleanor with a frown.

'I must have dozed in my chair before it happened,' he said. 'If I was already asleep then I would not have been aware of it.'

Eleanor nodded. 'That must be it.' Even so, it surprised her. Lucien did not seem the type of man to fall asleep in his chair. Still, she could think of no other explanation.

'The main thing is that no harm was done,' said Beddows. 'I'll go and see if the gas has dispersed. It's a wet night, and I don't want to leave the windows open for too long.'

'Do that,' said Lucien.

Beddows left the room.

'If you have recovered, then I should retire,' Eleanor said.

'Not yet.'

Something in his voice gave her pause.

'It was fortunate for me you couldn't sleep,' said Lucien. 'And even more fortunate that you were able to drag me from the room.'

'Fear gave me strength.'

'Fear?'

'When I saw you, I thought . . .' She swallowed. 'I thought you might be dead.'

He reached out and cupped her face in his hand.

'Poor Eleanor. This is the second time something like this has happened to you today. You found Kendrick, too.'

The feel of his thumb stroking her cheek was wonderful. She wanted to turn her head and kiss his hand. So worn out was she by the night's events that she only just managed to restrain herself.

'That was different. Mr Kendrick was an evil man, a blackmailer and a thief. But you . . .'

'Yes, Eleanor?'

His hand stilled.

'You . . .' She could not say what she really thought, so she said instead, 'You are none of those things.'

There was a soft look in his eyes that made her insides melt.

'Now that you are out of danger, I think I should retire,' she whispered.

She was becoming aware of the fact that she was alone with him, and that if she stayed she would succumb to his charm. In the evening, over dinner, it had been different. Then they had been companions. But now the relationship had altered. The atmosphere had become charged, and it was becoming increasingly difficult for her to concentrate.

He looked at her searchingly. Then, as if seeing the sense of what she said, he replied,

'Of course.'

He dropped his hand from her face.

She stood up and walked over to the door.

He rose, too.

'Before you go, I want to thank you.'

His words halted her. She turned round to see him standing in the candlelight, his dark hair falling in a lock across his forehead. His eyes were no longer steely, they were soft and warm. His cravat was awry and the top buttons of his shirt were undone, but his dishevelment only made her heart race even more.

Without knowing what she was doing she took a step towards him. He reached out his hand, and pushed her hair back from her face. He ran his hand over her unruly locks as they cascaded over her shoulders, and he stroked her cheek.

Then bending his head he kissed her softly on her lips.

It was as gentle as the brush of silk. She felt herself grow lightheaded with the ecstasy of it. She had never known a kiss could be like that. It took her breath away.

At last he lifted his mouth from hers, but it had been so wonderful that she was filled with an insane urge to stand on tiptoe and kiss him all over again. It was only with the greatest difficulty that she held herself back.

'You must be tired,' he said tenderly. 'You should go back to bed.'

She nodded mutely. It was all she could

manage. She could not trust herself to speak. With great difficulty, she turned round.

'If you were looking for something to read,' he said softly, 'the novels are by the door.'

She shook her head. A novel could not satisfy her now. No mere words could live up to the kiss she had just experienced. Perhaps she would not sleep. But, waking or sleeping, she would certainly dream.

Of him.

CHAPTER SIX

Eleanor's feelings were mixed as she went downstairs the following morning. She knew that today would take her away from Lucien, and she felt that it was just as well, because she had let him kiss her, and, even worse, she had felt no shame. She had been unable to resist his magnetism, and that being so, it was better that she was going away.

But a part of her, an irrational and yet important part, could not bear to be parted from him, and all the warmth and colour he had brought into her life.

As she reached the bottom of the flight of stairs she made a determined effort to concentrate on more practical affairs. There was no trace now of the smell that had filled the hall in the night. All the gas had gone, and the air in the house was fresh.

She went into the dining-room and was relieved to see that Lucien, who was sitting at the breakfast-table, looked none the worse for his experience of the night before.

'You're up early,' he said. He stood up as she entered the room.

'I was awake, so I thought I might as well rise.'

'You couldn't sleep?' he asked.

'No. Not very well.'

His eyes lit with an expression she could not fully understand. Was it understanding? Or compassion? Or something deeper? She was not sure. And yet she knew that it stirred feelings in her once again. Feelings it would be wiser to ignore.

'Never mind,' he said. 'Your adventures are over now. You will sleep well when you get home.'

Home! How strange it seemed to think of it. Life there was so calm and well-ordered. It was a complete contrast to the life she had known over the last few days. And yet for some reason she did not agree with Lucien, that she would sleep well once she returned. Her adventures might be over, but they had changed her. She was no longer the Eleanor Grantham who had left Bath a few days ago. She was someone older, more experienced . . . and also more confused.

As she sat down at the table and unfolded a

napkin she realized that her feelings towards Lucien were a mass of conflicting emotions. She had been angry with him to begin with for holding up the stagecoach, but now that she understood his reasons her feelings had changed. He had not wanted to do it—she remembered his enigmatic words at the time, which now made sense: *sometimes these things are necessary.* He had done it, not for a wager or some other foolish reason, but to help his country and thereby save many lives.

In other ways, too, her feelings had started to change. She had discovered a softer side to his character, and she had come to realize they shared a strong rapport. They shared, too, a sense of humour, and the hours she had spent in his company had been the most exhilarating, the most fulfilling and the most enjoyable of her life.

But then, during the night, she had discovered something more again. That he mattered to her. Deeply. Because when she had seen him unconscious—when she had thought for one terrible moment that he could be dead—she had felt bereft. The depth of her feelings had alarmed her. How could she have such profound feelings for a man she had only just met? She did not know. But the fact remained that she did.

It was strange that Lucien, sitting across the table from her, had no idea what her feelings were. She did not even know what they were herself, but as she sought for an answer, one word leapt into the forefront of her mind.

Love.

She shook her head. No. It could not be. And yet that was the word that had pushed its way into her thoughts. She had not been looking for it. Indeed, at the age of six-and-twenty, she had been convinced that love had passed her by. But there it was, that idea, in her mind. Love.

She did not explore the thought further. No good could come of it. In a few hours' time she would get on a stagecoach and never see Lucien again.

'What is it?' he asked, throwing her a quizzical look.

Startled out of her thoughts, she blushed.

'Oh . . . that is to say, I don't know what you mean.'

He regarded her closely. 'You looked suddenly . . . bereft.'

'Did I? I mean, no, how absurd. Why should I be bereft? I have done what I set out to do. I am overjoyed.'

He looked at her searchingly, and then to her relief he allowed the matter to drop.

'Here.' He poured her a cup of hot chocolate and handed her a plate of hot rolls. 'You need to keep your strength up.'

She took the chocolate and drank it down, but she did so without enjoyment. She had no appetite and ate only to give herself enough energy to face the coming journey.

'When you have finished, there is someone I want you to meet,' said Lucien.

Eleanor looked at him enquiringly.

'The disturbance last night has changed things,' he said. He hesitated. 'There's just a possibility that we were seen leaving Mr Kendrick's house. In case we were, and in case it puts you in danger, I want you to have someone with you, for protection. Don't worry, the man I've chosen is very discreet. He won't speak to you on your journey, or notice you in any way. In fact, he will seem like just another passenger on the stagecoach. Nevertheless, he'll be there if you need him.'

Eleanor was surprised. His fear that they might have been seen seemed very sudden. Unless . . .

She put down her cup. 'You're not convinced that the incident last night with the gas was an accident.'

He did not reply at once. Instead he looked at her, as if wondering what to say. Then, seeming to decide that he should tell her the truth, he said, 'No. I think it might have been an act of sabotage.'

Eleanor nodded. The same thought had occurred to her.

'But how was it done?' she asked.

'I'm not sure.'

'Do you think it was an attempt to kill you, so that the military documents could be stolen back again?' she asked.

'It's possible.'

'And have they been taken?' she asked practically.

He frowned. 'No.'

'Then why was it done?'

'I don't know. But remember, it's no more than an idea. Gas is still in its infancy, and not very reliable. It might have blown out by accident after all. Even so, I'm not taking any chances. As soon as you've finished your breakfast I'll introduce you to Cooper. He will make sure you are safe.'

Eleanor finished her hot rolls and chocolate, then Lucien rang the bell.

A minute later a burly man entered the room.

'Miss Grantham, this is Cooper,' said Lucien. 'Cooper, this is the young lady you are going to be protecting.'

Eleanor looked Cooper up and down. He was enormous, being well over six feet tall, and he was built like an ox.

'Miss Grantham,' he said, making her a bow.

Eleanor returned his greeting. Despite his enormous size she felt safe with him, and she was touched that Lucien had thought of providing her with a bodyguard.

'He will remain with you until I am sure there is no further danger. Perhaps you can find him something to do around the house?

Something that will not arouse suspicion?'

Eleanor nodded. 'I will think of something.'

His eyes held hers. There was something warm in them, and something unfathomable. Did he feel anything at the parting? she wondered. Just for a moment she thought he did.

And then he spoke. 'Now it is time for you to go.'

Eleanor glanced at the clock. Her coach would be leaving shortly. She gathered her things, and then Lucien saw her to the door.

'I will not be coming to the coaching inn with you,' he said. 'It's a busy place, and I will certainly be recognized. As the stage is going to Bath, there is a chance you will be recognized too. One of your neighbours, perhaps, might be on the coach. If so, being seen with me, unchaperoned, would ruin your reputation.'

Eleanor nodded. She knew that what he said made sense.

He took her hand, and then bending his head he kissed it.

She treasured the moment.

And then she was leaving. Saying her farewells, going out of the door, descending the steps, walking to the coaching inn, buying her ticket, taking her place in the stage. And saying goodbye to London, and everything she valued in it.

Once she had gone, Lucien stood looking at

the door for a very long time.

*   *   *

The coach made its way west. Cooper, sitting on the seat opposite Eleanor, was guarding her conscientiously. He had already scared away an eager young gentleman who had tried to engage her in conversation, and he had politely suggested that a disreputable-looking man who had winked at her would be happier sitting on the roof.

Eleanor, looking at the countryside as it rolled past, saw none of it. She was lost in her own thoughts, remembering the moment when Lucien had kissed her the night before. It had meant nothing to him, of course, but it had meant a great deal to her.

But it would not do to encourage such thoughts. Her relationship with Lucien was over now, and she would not see him again.

At the thought, her spirits sank still further. She had at last met a man who had stirred her in ways she had never known existed and she had seen, through him, a glimpse of a brighter, richer life. But it was beyond her reach.

Perhaps I will meet someone else who will make me feel that way, she told herself bracingly. Now I know such feelings exist, I might rediscover them at some future date.

But she did not believe it.

It was not as if she had never met any other

148

men. When her parents had been alive they had often entertained, and after that there had been Arabella's London Season. True, she herself had been nothing but a chaperon at the time, but she had still attended numerous balls, parties and routs and had had an opportunity to meet many gentlemen. But none of them had interested her. Until she had met Lucien.

She must not think of it. Dwelling on the situation would only make things worse. She must think of other things. Fortunately, Arabella's wedding would soon be upon her, and she would be busy until then, helping her sister to prepare for the big day. And afterwards . . . well, perhaps she would take a holiday. She had enough savings for a few days at the seaside, if she did not travel too far.

Pretending she had been cheered by this thought she focused her eyes on the scenery and did her best to enjoy the view.

*   *   *

'I've checked everywhere,' said Beddows, 'and there's no sign of a break-in.'

He was reporting back to Lucien, having examined every door and window in the house, but Lucien did not reply.

He was thinking of Eleanor, reflecting that by now she would be safely on the coach. As he thought of her intelligent face he knew he would never have forgiven himself if anything had happened to her. She had touched something inside him that he had not known he possessed. Women had come and gone in his life. He had regarded them as pleasant distractions from the grim reality of warfare, or the tedium of Society. But Eleanor was different. He did not know why it should be. She was spirited, that was true, and courageous, but those aspects of her character, whilst explaining the admiration he felt for her, could not explain the deeper feelings he had experienced whilst in her company.

He gave a wicked smile as he thought of the physical attraction he felt for her. It was too potent to be denied. She was not conventionally beautiful, and taller than the present fashion demanded, but she had fascinating eyes and a tempting mouth. Besides, the chemistry that existed between them was not dependent on beauty; it operated on a far deeper level.

But then the smile faded, to be replaced by a thoughtful expression. Because, whilst physical attraction was something he understood, the protective feelings he felt towards her were new. They were born, not of a good upbringing, but of a deep-rooted instinct to protect his mate.

And there he went again, thinking of mates! What had come over him? He had resisted every effort ever made to leg-shackle him. He had fought off Society's most determined mamas, and yet here he was, thinking of leg-shackling himself. Only for some reason it didn't seem like shackling. It seemed like joining. Joining, merging, becoming one. And then splitting again, separating into many parts, small parts, growing parts—Good God! He was thinking of his nurseries again! And not just his nurseries. His house, his garden, his life, all full of rough-and-tumble children wrestling with puppies and scratching the table, children with black hair and hazel eyes . . .

'Hrrrm.'

Beddows cleared his throat, and Lucien was brought back to the present.

He shook his head to clear away the images that had been besetting him. He had no business thinking of nurseries, or marriage, or anything else, until Kendrick's killer had been caught, and until he was convinced that last night's accident had not been anything more sinister.

'You were saying?' he asked.

'I said I've checked the house,' said Beddows, repeating his earlier phrase. He had guessed, quite rightly, that Lucien had not heard a word.

Lucien became more vigorous. Withdrawing his thoughts from Eleanor with difficulty he turned to the matter in hand.

'And? Has there been a forced entry?'

151

'No,' said Beddows.

Lucien frowned.

'You don't think it was an accident, then, the gas blowing out?' asked Beddows.

'It could have been. But it seems too much of a coincidence that it should have happened on the day I retrieved the documents.'

'But they are still here?'

'They are. But would they have been if Elean—Miss Grantham hadn't come downstairs? I don't think so. Yet if it wasn't an accident, how did the perpetrator get in? You've checked the house,' said Lucien thoughtfully, then asked, 'but how thoroughly? Have you checked the attics?'

'There's no way in through the attics,' said Beddows.

'Make sure,' said Lucien. 'If someone got in here to blow out the gas when I'd fallen asleep, then I want to know how they did it. And I want to make sure they can't get in again. Not that I'll be spending the night here for some time. I have to get these back to where they belong.'

He glanced at the documents lying on the table. 'Even so, I want to make sure the house is secure.'

'Then I'll check the attics,' said Beddows, 'and let you know what I find.'

Once Beddows had departed, Lucien picked up the papers, then donned his greatcoat and headed off to meet the general. His business

152

was too important to be delayed. And besides, the fresh air would help to blow the lingering thoughts of Eleanor out of his mind.

At least, he hoped it would.

*   *   *

Eleanor felt her spirits lift as she saw Bath spread out below her, looking peaceful and serene in the September afternoon. Its buildings of golden stone looked warm and inviting. The blue ribbon of the River Avon snaked its way past and between them, disappearing now and again as it ran beneath an elegant bridge before emerging, sparkling, into the sunlight.

As the coach began to descend the hill Eleanor could see the gardens. Despite the lateness of the season, they were filled with colourful flowers. There, too, were the promenades. Although Bath had declined in recent years and was not the fashionable resort it had been when Eleanor, her mother and her sister had removed there ten years before, it still had an elegance and charm that rendered it lovely in her eyes.

She thought of the day when she and her family had first arrived. They had had to economize, having suffered a reduction in their income following her father's death, and so they had settled on the outskirts of Bath where it was possible to live economically. The waters had been another attraction. Mrs Grantham had been in low spirits, and the family had hoped the health-giving properties of the waters would be of use to her. Daily visits to the Pump Room had followed, but unfortunately their mother had at last died and the two girls had been left alone. Since when Eleanor had done everything in her power to look after Arabella.

The coach now began to pass fashionable ladies and gentlemen who were strolling along arm in arm. The ladies, gay in their feathered bonnets and colourful pelisses, were holding parasols to shelter their complexions from the sun. There were children walking with their nurses, and ragged urchins playing in the street.

At last the coach turned into the yard of the coaching inn. There was a hustle and bustle as it drew to a halt. All was noise and confusion. Private carriages were coming and going, some of them being driven by coachmen and some being driven by dandified young gentlemen. Elegant ladies and gentlemen were picking their way across the yard, going either to or from the inn, and servants were overseeing the stowing or unloading of luggage. Boys were running errands and stray dogs were getting in their way, but Eleanor scarcely noticed it. The noise and confusion passed her by, and as she climbed out of the coach she was just pleased to be back in Bath.

Going carefully so as to avoid the postboys, ostlers and footmen who were running to and fro, she made her way out of the yard. Cooper, as arranged, followed unobtrusively behind her. Then she turned and headed for home.

It was not long before she reached the house she and Arabella shared on the outskirts of Bath. It was a small building but it was attractive, being built of Bath's glowing golden stone. Its long windows reached almost to the ground, and it was surrounded by a generous garden.

Eleanor went through the gate and walked up the path, ignoring the weeds that sprang up here and there. She had tried to keep the garden tidy, but it was a never-ending task, particularly at this time of year, when leaves were constantly falling from the trees. She approached the door, with its shining brasses, and as it was the maid's day off she let herself in.

As she opened the front door she smiled. It was good to be home. Her eyes wandered over the familiar hall. The warm tones of the biscuit paintwork contrasted with the white panelling, and created a welcoming feel. A console table was set against the wall to her left, and above it hung a gilded mirror, whilst next to them was a long-case clock.

There was a letter on the console table, addressed to Arabella. She recognized her own handwriting. It was the letter she had sent from Lydia and Frederick's house, explaining her absence, but now that she had arrived home before Arabella there was no further need for it. She picked it up. She would rather explain matters to her sister in person.

Her eyes drifted through the open door on the left of the hall into an elegant dining-room. It held a mahogany table and chairs, and had gold drapes framing the window. A few good pictures hung on the walls. Then her eyes drifted back across the hall to look into the sitting-room. A floral sofa, together with two easy chairs, were arranged around the fireplace, and an escritoire took advantage of the light beneath the window.

She undid the strings of her bonnet and laid it on the console table, then went upstairs. Her bedroom was welcoming, with the sun streaming in at the windows. The patchwork quilt, which had been carefully stitched by Arabella and herself, glowed in warm colours on the bed. Two watercolours of the house, painted by her mother, hung above it.

She took off her cloak, then patted her hair into place in front of the mirror before going downstairs. She went through into the kitchen, and was pleased to see that Molly had left everything neat, clean and tidy. The copper pots and pans were gleaming on the dresser, and the large table had been well scrubbed.

She set about lighting the fire. Although the sunshine was pouring in through the window, it was cold.

Fortunately, everything was laid out ready. The coal-bucket was standing next to the large dresser, and it was full to overflowing. She had just picked it up when there came a knock at the back door. Cooper, who had been following at a discreet distance, had at last arrived. She put down the coal-bucket and let him in.

'I was just about to light a fire,' she said, as she saw his eyes drift to her dirty hands.

'I can do that for you, miss.' Without waiting for a reply he took off his coat, rolled up his sleeves, and said, 'You leave it to me.'

She smiled. 'Thank you.' She had been wondering what to do with Cooper, but now she knew. She was happy for him to light the fires, as it had never been one of her favourite tasks!

He set to with a will. He lit the paper that lined the grate and waited for it to flare up, setting fire to the twigs that were piled on top of it. Once they were burning thoroughly he poured on the coal.

'You're very good at it,' she said, as she rinsed her hands at the sink.

'My old mother always used to say I laid the best fire in the county,' said Cooper with pride.

'I can see we will be very glad to have you with us. It was good of Lord Silverton to arrange for you to stay,' she added a trifle awkwardly. It was not easy for her to talk about Lucien, but she could not avoid all mention of him, particularly with Cooper, and so she tried to sound at ease.

'Ah, he's a good man,' agreed Cooper.

Eleanor felt a pang at this praise from one who obviously knew him well. Lucien was in every way someone she wanted to be with, and yet she would have to resign herself to the fact that she would never see him again. How she was going to do it she did not know. But she must at least attempt it, if she was not to drive herself mad.

Resolutely turning her thoughts into more practical channels, she said, 'I am not sure how to explain your presence to my sister when she arrives. Unfortunately, I don't think she will believe that you are a new footman. We haven't had a footman for years, as we haven't been able to afford one. And even if we could afford one, I'm afraid you don't look the part.'

Cooper smiled widely: anyone who looked less like a footman would be hard to imagine! In both looks and manner he was too rough and rugged for an indoor servant.

'Even so, I'm not leaving you alone, miss,' rumbled Cooper. 'His lordship's instructions were clear. I'm to keep an eye on you, and make sure no harm befalls you, until he tells me it's all right for me to leave.'

'And I'm glad of it. I must admit I will feel safer for having you here. Although I'm sure I'm in no danger,' she added.

'Just so, miss. But it's better not to take chances. Kendrick was a nasty piece of work, and the villains he mixed with were even nastier. If they happened to see you leaving his house in Pall Mall on the night of the murder, they might take it into their heads to silence you, just in case you'd seen anything. But as long as you go through the next few weeks without anything happening I reckon you'll be safe. If anyone saw you leaving the house, they'll make their move quickly or not at all.'

Eleanor nodded. 'Still, I'm not sure what to tell Arabella. I don't want to worry her with the truth, but I must tell her something. She will be home soon.'

For the moment she could not think of a solution to the problem.

Glancing round the room, she said, 'Would you like a cup of tea?'

'Thank you, miss,' said Cooper, sitting back on his heels as the fire began to blaze. 'I'll put the kettle on.'

'You know how to brew tea as well?' she asked with raised eyebrows: it seemed there was nothing this giant of a man couldn't do!

'I can turn my hands to most things if needs be,' he said comfortably.

Eleanor relinquished the task of making the tea and wandered over to the window. She sighed. Although the house was looking just as it had when she had left it, the garden was very much untidier. The autumn leaves had been busily fluttering from the trees, and the garden was awash with them. It would be an endless job for the next few weeks to clear them up, which was a positive nuisance as she had so much to do.

An idea struck her. 'Can you turn your hand to gardening?' she asked Cooper.

He brightened. 'Oh, yes. I like a bit of gardening, miss. I've always been an outdoor sort, rather than an indoor.'

'Good. Then that's settled. I'll tell Arabella that I've hired you to help outside for the next few weeks. We often hire someone to help with the leaves at this time of year, so she won't find it strange.'

'A good idea, miss,' said Cooper, handing her a cup of tea. 'I can keep an eye on you and the house without anyone being the wiser.' Eleanor took her tea into the parlour whilst Cooper, true to his masquerade as a gardener, remained with his cup in the kitchen.

It was a good thing he did, because no sooner had Eleanor finished her drink than a carriage rolled up outside the house. She recognised it as the one belonging to Arabella's friend. Sure enough, out stepped Arabella, handed down by one of Mary's footmen.

Eleanor smiled with pride as she watched her sister trip up the path. Arabella's golden hair glinted in the sunshine, and her big blue eyes lit up her pretty heart-shaped face. Her dainty figure was adorable, and it was not surprising that half the young men in London had been in love with her.

A lesser girl would have become spoilt. But Arabella had retained her sweet and affectionate nature, and was as lovely inside as she was out. True, she was rather timid, and she was inclined to let others make decisions for her, but what did it matter? She had Charles to make her decisions for her now, and he was a trustworthy man.

For Charles, too, the match seemed perfect. He was kindly and courteous, and he liked Arabella's helplessness, as it gave him an opportunity to look after her.

Arabella was wearing a pale-pink pelisse, a gift from Charles, which matched her delicate complexion. Beneath it she wore a dress of the finest white muslin. Even so, there was a faint cloud on her face, and it did Eleanor good to know that she could remove it, setting her sister's mind at rest about the letters.

She went to the open the front door.

'Oh, Eleanor, it is lovely to see you,' said Arabella, hugging Eleanor warmly. 'I missed you!'

The footman, having followed Arabella from the carriage, carried her valise inside and then departed, leaving the two young ladies to catch up on all their news.

'Did you enjoy yourself?' asked Eleanor.

'Yes. It was lovely to see Mary again.'

Arabella hesitated. 'And you? Did you manage to speak to Mr Kendrick?'

'I did.' Eleanor linked her arm through her sister's and led her into the sitting-room. 'You have nothing more to worry about. I have managed to retrieve your letters.'

Arabella's face was flooded with relief. 'You have? Oh, that's wonderful. Thank you.'

Her words were heartfelt, and were accompanied by an impulsive hug.

'It has taken such a load off my mind,' she went on. 'I was so afraid I had done the wrong thing by telling you. If he had been horrid to you I would have felt awful.' She looked at Eleanor anxiously. 'I hope he was not too horrid?'

'No,' said Eleanor reassuringly. She had no intention of telling Arabella about the adventures and trials she had endured. All Arabella needed to know was that the letters had been successfully retrieved.

Arabella gave a heartfelt sigh.

She was about to sit down when she noticed Cooper through the window. She turned to Eleanor enquiringly.

'I have hired a man to help with the garden,' said Eleanor. 'The leaves are such a nuisance at this time of year.'

Arabella nodded. 'Good. It will be nice to have it tidy again.'

'Now,' said Eleanor, as she sat down opposite her sister, 'tell me all about your visit.'

*   *   *

To Eleanor's relief, the ncxt few weeks passed quickly. It was a busy time. and although she had not been able to banish Lucien from her mind she was at least able to concentrate well enough to help Arabella with her preparations for the wedding. There were many things Arabella needed to buy, and the shops in Milsom Street provided the perfect place to find them. Gloves, hats, shawls and scarves were gradually added to Arabella's trousseau. Then there was the friseur to consult, and the modiste to visit, so that all in all there was never a minute to spare.

Unbeknownst to Arabella, they had a shadow when they went on their errands, for Cooper followed at a discreet distance to make sure they were safe.

'My dear Miss Arabella,' gushed Madame Dupas one fine morning as the two ladies made their way into her salon. ' 'ow good it is to see you. And Miss Grantham, you are both very welcome.'

She clapped her hands, sending her assistants scurrying into the workroom to bring out the two young ladies' gowns.

The gowns were both being paid for out of a legacy left to Eleanor and Arabella by an aged aunt some two years previously. The same

163

legacy had paid for Arabella's London Season. There had been enough left over to provide Arabella with her wedding finery, and Eleanor with a new gown for the wedding.

'Oh! It looks wonderful!' gasped Arabella, as Madame Dupas held up her wedding-gown.

'Try it on,' said Eleanor.

With the help of Madame Dupas's assistants, Arabella slipped off her muslin walking-dress, and then slipped on her wedding-gown. It was beautiful. The white silk underskirt shimmered beneath the gauze overskirt. The bodice was strewn with seed-pearls, whilst the short puffed sleeves were so delicate they appeared to be made of gossamer.

'Bella, you look beautiful,' said Eleanor.

'Do you think Charles will like it?' asked Arabella, her eyes shining.

'Charles will love it,' Eleanor assured her.

'You 'ave lost weight,' said Madame Dupas with a tutting noise. 'You brides! You are so excited, you forget to eat. You must keep your strength up. But see, I take a tiny tuck 'ere, and a little tuck there,'—she adjusted the gown with pins—'and it is done.'

Arabella turned round to see the back of the gown. A ribbon bow ornamented the high waist, and a short train trailed elegantly behind her.

'It's wonderful,' breathed Arabella.

'You come back in one week, and I 'ave it

finished,' said Madame Dupas, making a last-minute alteration to the hem.

Arabella slipped out of her gown, and then it was Eleanor's turn. She was to be Arabella's chief attendant, and had chosen a beautiful gown from the pages of the *Lady's Monthly Magazine.* She had shown the engraving to Madame Dupas, and wondered how accurately Madame Dupas had been able to copy it.

As she slipped it on, she realized it was perfect. In style it was similar to Arabella's gown, with a high waist and short puffed sleeves, but there the similarity ended. The sleeves, bodice and overskirt were made of the finest muslin in a becoming shade of dusky pink, set off by an underskirt of white silk. The dusky colour suited her complexion, bringing out the warmth of her cheeks.

'You look lovely,' Arabella told her. 'You must thread a pink ribbon through your hair on the day. It will be just the thing.'

Madame Dupas made one or two minor alterations, and then they set out for home. Whilst Arabella chattered happily away, Eleanor could not prevent her thoughts from wandering to Lucien. She had tried not to think of him, but his black hair and blue eyes kept returning to disturb her thoughts.

'. . . although perhaps the yellow . . . are you all right, Eleanor?' asked Arabella.

'Hm? Yes, of course. Why?'

'It's just that you seem distracted,' said

Arabella. Her face fell. 'It must be very boring for you, listening to me rattle on like this.'

'Not at all,' said Eleanor, giving her arm a squeeze.

'Oh, good, because I wanted to talk to you about the honeymoon. Charles and I have still not decided where to go, whether to go to the Lakes, or whether to venture further afield, to Scotland.'

The two ladies crossed the road, then Arabella said, 'Are you sure you won't come with us, Eleanor?'

'Quite sure.'

Although it was the custom for brides to take a sister or other female relative on honeymoon with them, Eleanor knew that Arabella and Charles were very much in love and would not need a third person to keep them company.

'What do you think?' asked Arabella, as they continued on their way. 'I would like to see Scotland, but I think it might be too far.'

'It would certainly be tiring,' said Eleanor. 'And you cannot be away for too long because of Charles's responsibilities.'

'Yes, I think you are right. I think perhaps we had better go to the Lakes instead.'

They were now approaching their own house, and went inside. Arabella was soon knee-deep in boxes and paper as she unwrapped her purchases. She was just about to try on a particularly fetching bonnet when a curricle drew up outside the house.

'Oh! Here is Charles!' she exclaimed, dropping her bonnet. 'Isn't it funny, we had to go all the way to London to meet each other, when we had unknowingly lived no more than twenty miles from each other all our lives. I am so glad he is here.'

She ran to the door. She made a charming picture as she stood on tiptoe to kiss Charles on the cheek, and then she drew him into the sitting-room.

He was a manly gentleman, tall and fair, with an elegant manner. His clothes were well cut without being ostentatious, and he wore them with an air of ease.

'My dear Charles,' said Eleanor, greeting him. 'Welcome.'

'Eleanor,' said Charles warmly, returning her greeting. He looked at her more closely. 'You're looking a little peaky,' he said. 'I hope you two young ladies have been getting enough fresh air.'

'I noticed it myself,' said Arabella. 'I am afraid I must have been working Eleanor too hard, making her accompany me on all my shopping trips.'

'Nonsense!' declared Eleanor. 'I am very well. But Arabella tells me you have not yet decided between the Lake District and Scotland for your honeymoon,' she said, changing the subject. 'Do you think you will have time to go north of the border?'

'I think it unlikely,' said Charles. He turned to Arabella lovingly. 'I don't want to tire my new bride.'

'Oh, Charles,' said Arabella, blushing becomingly.

'And to that end, my dear, I have been thinking. I have decided we should have a day of rest after the wedding before setting off on our honeymoon. After all the celebrations, and then the wedding itself, you are bound to be fatigued.'

Eleanor agreed. Charles's family, once they had accustomed themselves to the idea of his marrying a penniless young lady, had decided to celebrate in lavish style. They had arranged a series of celebrations for the week leading up to the wedding, culminating in a grand ball. They had originally organized it for the night before the wedding, but Charles had put his foot down, and now it was to take place two days before the wedding. That way, Arabella would have a quiet day in which to prepare herself for the ceremony. Charles's latest idea, to delay their start on their journey northwards, also seemed a good idea. The wedding itself would be very grand, and then would come the lavish wedding breakfast. By the time it was over, Arabella would be exhausted.

'I think you're right,' said Arabella. 'I must admit I was rather dreading having to travel so soon after having all that food and

168

champagne! I was worried the journey might make me ill.'

Charles laughed. 'It will be quite a wedding breakfast. My mother has been planning it for months. The Duke of Rainster is the only person who has declined, but it is not surprising as his health has been poor for some time. Lady Musgrave has replied at last—she's coming—and Lord Silverton, but—'

'Lord Silverton?' Eleanor was so startled to hear his name that the words were out before she could stop them.

Charles looked at her curiously. 'Yes. Lord Silverton. We were together at Eton, and then later at Oxford. Why?'

'Oh. No reason,' said Eleanor, colouring slightly.

It had never occurred to her that Lucien might be at the wedding, and yet she should have guessed. He was from an old and well-respected family, and he was a member of the *ton*. As such he would inevitably mix in the same circles as Charles.

'He went into the army after that, and I saw little of him,' went on Charles. 'This is a perfect opportunity to see him again. I hope he comes.' He smiled lovingly down at Arabella. 'I want to introduce him to my beautiful bride.'

Eleanor fought down her unruly feelings. Lucien's acceptance had nothing to do with her, she told herself. He simply wanted to attend the wedding of one of his old school-friends. Even so, unwise as it was, she could not help her heart leaping at the thought of seeing him again.

CHAPTER SEVEN

The week of the wedding arrived at last. Since learning that Lucien would be attending, Eleanor had found it impossible to settle to anything, but at last she was getting ready for the ball.

The ball was being held at Charles's parents' estate, Longbridge Grange, not far from Bath. Eleanor and Arabella had been collected by a private coach in the afternoon. A suite of rooms had been made over to them, and they had been given the services of a bevy of maids to help them dress.

'Just think,' said Arabella nervously, 'this is how my life is going to be from now on.'

'Don't worry, Bella.' Eleanor placed a reassuring hand on Arabella's arm. 'Remember, you will be the mistress of your own house. It will be up to you how many maids you employ. You don't have to be surrounded by quite so many.'

Arabella was comforted. 'That's true. I could appoint some nice young girl that I could train up to be my lady's maid,' she said, relaxing a little: the maids at the Grange were all rather daunting!

'That's right. Someone you get on with, and who understands your ways,' said Eleanor encouragingly.

Arabella smiled, her confidence restored, and they turned their attention to putting on their gowns.

The gowns had been bought for Arabella's London Season and had been made by a skilled modiste, so that even at tonight's splendid gathering they would not look out of place. Fortunately no one in Bath had seen them, so no one would know they were not new. Arabella's gown was exquisite. Made of pale-blue silk, it had a high waist and a scooped neckline, and its bodice was scattered with brilliants.

'I've always liked you in that dress,' said Eleanor approvingly. 'It's just right for this evening.'

'Your gloves, miss,' said one of the maids, holding out a pair of long white evening gloves to Arabella.

Arabella pulled on the gloves, then picked up her fan just as the clock struck the hour.

'Oh, we're late,' said Arabella. 'Do you mind if I go down without you? I have to receive our guests when they arrive.'

'Of course not. I'll be down directly,' said Eleanor.

Arabella tripped out of the room, leaving

Eleanor to finish her own *toilette.*

Eleanor's gown was no less beautiful than Arabella's. As Arabella's chaperon in London her appearance had been important, and so she had had a number of ball-gowns made. This one was her favourite. It was made of white satin, and it had a gold overskirt which matched the gold bodice. The colour suited her. It made her eyes appear more hazel and less brown, and brightened the colour of her hair. Its high waist made the most of her figure, and its short puffed sleeves showed off the smoothness of her arms.

She glanced at her hair. It had been arranged into an elaborate style. The duchess's maids were skilled at dressing hair, and they had replaced the simple knot she usually wore with a chignon. After arranging it, they had plaited a loose strand of her hair and wrapped it round the chignon's base to give an added touch of elegance, before arranging soft ringlets around her face. As a final touch, they had threaded a gold ribbon through the plait.

As Eleanor picked up her fan she was feminine enough to be pleased that she was looking her best.

The maids stood aside, and she went downstairs. As she did so, she wondered whether Lucien would be at the ball. He had not attended any of the other wedding festivities. She had hoped to see him at the firework display, and the soirée, and the other enjoyments the duchess had arranged, but he had not been there. But it was now only two days before the wedding, and perhaps, if he was already in Bath, he would come to the ball. Yet even if he did, she must not refine too much upon it. Their acquaintance had been brief, and though it had meant a great deal to her, she had no reason to believe it had meant anything to him.

She went into the ballroom. It looked magnificent. Large chandeliers hung from the ceiling and gilded mirrors lined the walls. In between them stood marble pillars, with exquisite flower arrangements displayed on their tops. The musicians were sitting at one end of the room, just putting the finishing touches to tuning their instruments. Eleanor's eyes ran over the people standing and talking around the sides of the room. And then stopped. For there, at the far end, was Lucien.

Talking to Miss Aireton.

Miss Aireton was one of Bath's greatest beauties. Her flaxen hair was set off by her huge green eyes, and her curvaceous figure was perfect. As if this was not enough, she was also an heiress, and she would have a dowry of £20,000.

Eleanor's spirits sank. Miss Aireton was evidently saying something amusing, and Lucien looked to be thoroughly enjoying himself. Still, it came as a timely reminder that she must not presume too much upon their acquaintance, nor read into it anything that did not exist. When she danced with Lucien . . . *if* she danced with Lucien . . . she must remember that.

'Ah, there you are, Miss Grantham,' said the duchess, sailing towards her with all the majesty of a royal frigate. 'Allow me to present Lord Accrington.'

Since realizing that Charles was serious about marrying Arabella, and that there was no chance of her preventing it, the duchess had wisely decided to accept the situation and had welcomed Arabella into the family. That welcome had been extended to Eleanor, and it was clear that the duchess meant to help her to marry well, for if dear Arabella's sister was to marry a nobleman then it would provide Arabella with a titled relative.

Eleanor greeted the young lord politely, as she greeted every other young gentleman whom the duchess introduced to her. Her hand was sought for almost every dance of the evening, and her card was soon nearly full.

'And now let me introduce you to Lord Silverton.'

Eleanor's heart leapt in her breast. There was the black hair and the blue eyes she had dreamed of, the dimpled chin, and the lips she longed to touch.

'We've met,' he said.

The smile he gave Eleanor set her heart racing. Despite all her best intentions she

174

could not help remembering the way his body had felt when it had been crushed against hers: the strength in his arms, and the power of his chest. And by the smouldering look in his eye, he was remembering it too.

'Have you indeed?' asked the duchess, looking from one to the other of them. 'In that case you can take Miss Grantham on to the floor for the cotillion. It's just about to begin.'

'Your wish is my command,' said Lucien to the duchess.

'It never has been before,' she snorted. 'You were always too busy going your own way.' She gave him a curious look, then said, 'The musicians are striking up. You'd better hurry.'

Lucien offered Eleanor his arm.

Resting her hand lightly on it, she could feel the heat of him through his tailcoat, and as he led her to the floor he was so close that she could smell the scent of his cologne.

Taking a moment to steady her pulse and control the most noticeable of her reactions to his touch, she said, 'I didn't realize you knew the duchess.'

'I spent one of my summer holidays with Charles when I was a boy,' he said. 'It was an . . . interesting . . . experience. The duchess decided we needed dancing lessons. I remember her telling me it was the hallmark of every civilized gentleman, but—'

'But you did not wish to take them?' Eleanor smiled.

'I was more of a soldier than a dancer, even in those days,' he agreed. 'But when I grew up I realized she was right. Being able to dance is the hallmark of a gentleman. It has taken me until now to realize that it can also be a pleasure.'

Eleanor felt a broad smile break out on her face. She could not help it. Even so, she knew she must not encourage him. Encouraging him would be dangerous.

'You should not say such things, Lucien,' she said.

'Ah!' His voice was full of satisfaction. 'You remember my name.'

'That is, I mean to say, Lord Silverton,' she corrected herself hastily.

She had not meant to call him Lucien, it had just slipped out. In London, with no one to hear her, it had not mattered. But it was quite another thing to call him Lucien here. Fortunately, the other dancers had not heard what she had said, and her indiscretion had not been noticed.

'Too late,' he said. 'The damage is done.' His eyes glowed as he looked down at her.

'Please, speak of something else,' she begged him.

'Very well. You look wonderful,' he said.

His compliment made her tingle from head to foot. She could not help being pleased that he had noticed her gown. When he had seen her on previous occasions she had been wearing her worn and shabby muslin, but now he was seeing her in an elegant creation, and by the way he was drinking her in, his words were genuine.

'Your hairstyle is new as well. It suits you,' he said.

His eyes lingered on the elaborate chignon, and the soft tendrils that had been teased out around her face.

She was delighted that he had noticed, and yet at the same time his comments made her feel vulnerable. What did he mean by it? If in fact he meant anything at all?

Replying lightly, she said, 'As befits the sister of the bride.'

His eyes danced, as though he understood why she had made such a light reply, and feeling she must turn the conversation into a less intimate channel, she made a remark on the elegance of the room. To her relief, he allowed her to turn the conversation, and made a similar remark before saying how happy Arabella and Charles looked.

'She seems a sweet girl,' he said, glancing at Arabella, who had now entered the ballroom, having greeted all her guests. 'I must admit, when you told me about the letters, I wondered—'

'Whether she was a scheming hussy, who had had a string of admirers before managing to catch a future duke?' asked Eleanor with a smile, seeing where his thoughts had been tending.

He laughed. 'The thought had crossed my mind. But that is obviously not the case. I see now why you were so determined to protect her. She's very lovely, but she lacks your spirit. When I was introduced to her I realized that she is little more than a child.'

'You underestimate her,' said Eleanor. 'But even so, I'm glad she has Charles to take care of her.'

His eyes returned to her own. 'You should have someone to take care of you,' he said meaningfully.

She swallowed. There was something intimate about his glance. It was as though his eyes did not rest on the outside of her, but looked inside her, seeing through to the depths of her being.

'I . . .' She stopped. Her mouth had suddenly become dry, and the words would not come out. She tried again. 'I do not need anyone. As you say, I have enough spirit to look after myself.'

His hand took hers as a part of the dance and she tingled all over. She hoped he would not notice her reaction, but the look on his face told her that he most definitely had.

'Eleanor—'

'I don't think you should call me that,' she said, relieved that a loud series of chords from the orchestra had hidden his indiscretion.

'Why not?' he asked teasingly. 'It's your

name.'

'It will raise—'

'Expectations?' he asked.

Her heart skipped a beat. What could he be meaning by talking to her like this? He sounded as though he *wanted* to raise expectations.

But before the interesting conversation could continue, the dance came to an end.

Lucien bowed and, as custom dictated, Eleanor curtsied. Then he led her from the floor. He took her to the side of the room where, although surrounded by people, they were effectively alone. They knew no one in their vicinity, and would not be called upon to make conversation with anyone but themselves.

'Eleanor,' he began, when a loud cry of, 'Silverton! Aha! There you are,' interrupted them.

From across the crowded ballroom, Lady Dalrymple was hailing Lucien.

'I want to introduce you to my daughter,' said the countess, coming forcefully forward with an insipid young lady in tow. As she arrived she gave Eleanor a glance that said, *What is a nobody like you doing here? You should be polishing the furniture, instead of monopolizing a wealthy earl who would make a perfect husband for my daughter!*

Lucien threw Eleanor a speaking look, but then turned towards the countess. 'Charmed.'

Good manners forbade him from giving the countess a set-down, but after exchanging a few pleasantries he said, 'If you will excuse me, I have promised to fetch Miss Grantham an ice.'

'I didn't know you had done any such thing,' said Eleanor humorously as the countess reluctantly departed.

'Perhaps not, but I was going to. Would you care for an ice? Or perhaps you would prefer a glass of champagne?'

'An ice would be very welcome,' she admitted.

'Good.' He smiled. It was a caressing smile, and heated her insides. It seemed she was going to need an ice after all!

He returned a few minutes later with the confection.

'I did not know you would be here tonight,' she said as she took a spoonful of ice.

'I wasn't sure myself. I had . . . things to do.'

She nodded. Her thoughts returned to the sombre events that must have been occupying Lucien since last they met.

'Have you caught Mr Kendrick's killer?' she asked.

'Not yet. We've rounded up a number of his contacts—it takes a chain of people to steal and then smuggle military documents out of the country—but so far they have all had convincing alibis for the time of the killing. His murderer still eludes us.'

Eleanor shivered. Although there had been no untoward incidents in Bath, no suspicious characters hovering outside the house or unexplained accidents, she was still aware that the dangers might not yet be over.

'You will not be taking Cooper away, then?'

'No.' Lucien looked round. 'He's not here tonight?'

'I could find no way to bring him. Charles's family would have wanted to know who he was. But there are so many footmen, gardeners, bootboys, stable hands and other sundry servants here that I knew I would be safe.'

Lucien nodded. 'You've managed to keep him with you at other times?'

'Yes. He's been very useful.' Her mood lightened. 'In fact, he's been working in the garden. It's never looked so tidy!'

'It seems Cooper has hidden talents! Still, I'm glad you have him to watch over you. Until we track down Kendrick's killer, I don't want to take any chances with your safety.'

She was warmed by his concern.

'Eleanor—' he began.

There was a new note in his voice, and Eleanor looked up to see him apparently in the grip of some strong emotion. 'Eleanor, I know now isn't the time, but—'

'Ah! Miss Grantham, there you are,' said Lord Accrington as he hurried up.

'Damn!' cursed Lucien under his breath.

'I've been looking for you all over the place,' continued Lord Accrington. 'I hope you haven't forgotten we're engaged for the next dance?'

Eleanor *had* forgotten, but it was very true, she was engaged to him for the next dance. She gave an inward sigh. She had no inclination whatsoever to dance with him, especially not now, but she had no choice. She had to take his arm.

'Lord Silverton,' she said, making him a curtsy.

'Miss Grantham,' he said, taking her empty ice-dish.

Then he turned his attention to Lord Accrington, favouring him with a look that had the young lord running his finger round his collar. 'Come, Miss Grantham,' said the poor young nobleman nervously, 'we must away.'

Eleanor forced herself to smile politely and reluctantly accompanied him on to the dance floor. It was not that Lord Accrington was unpleasant. Far from it. Once away from Lucien's presence he recovered his composure and entertained Eleanor with light and agreeable conversation. But he wasn't Lucien, and she had little pleasure in the dance. After dancing with Lord Accrington, her hand was claimed by three more partners, and she grew increasingly frustrated as it seemed she would not have any further opportunity to speak to Lucien. He interested her more than any other

182

man at the ball—he interested her more than any other man she had ever met—but circumstances conspired to keep them apart. Lucien was introduced to every eligible young lady at the ball, and she herself had to dance with any number of eligible young gentlemen. She hoped she might have a chance to speak to him at supper-time, but it was not to be. She was taken in by one of Charles's cousins, and Lucien was called upon to escort a countess.

After supper it was even worse. Not only did she have no opportunity to speak to Lucien, she did not even see him again until the evening had come to an end. But then, in the hall, whilst the guests were waiting for their carriages, Lucien broke away from a particularly determined mama and made his way to Eleanor's side.

'Miss Grantham,' he said with a bow. 'May I have the honour of calling on you tomorrow?'

He could say no more. Arabella and Charles were there, and a host of other guests. But it was enough.

Eleanor murmured, 'Delighted.'

'Good. I will call in the afternoon.'

There was a warmth in his voice that lit her up inside. And then, his attention being claimed by a particularly persistent dowager, he was forced to turn away.

As she returned home, Eleanor's thoughts were filled with happy visions of the following day. She had not expected to see Lucien again, but she had done so, and he had evidently not forgotten her. Quite the reverse. He wanted to see her. To speak to her. And he was to call on her the following afternoon.

As she leant back against the squabs her mind wandered down a number of different pathways, all of them exceedingly pleasant. It was something of importance he wanted to say, she was sure. There had been a tone in his voice that had made her guess . . . But she must not think about it. She must wait until tomorrow to find out what he had to say.

*   *   *

Eleanor was glad that she had a number of last-minute purchases to make for Arabella's wedding the following morning. It would help to pass the time until Lucien called. As soon as she had breakfasted she set out for the shops. There was a light breeze, but the sky was blue and fresh. She spent an enjoyable hour buying rosettes for Arabella's wedding slippers, as well as a dozen cambric handkerchiefs and a bottle of lavender water. She decided to take a turn round Sidney Gardens before going to the circulating library and borrowing an entertaining novel to read—it would give her something to occupy herself with until Lucien called. She had just entered the gardens when she heard a loud hail.

'Eleanor!'

184

She turned round to see Thomas, the young poet who had exchanged such indiscreet letters with Arabella, hurrying towards her. Eleanor noticed with amusement that he was dressed in typically flamboyant style. His cravat was ostentatiously tied, and his waistcoat gleamed with gold embroidery. He had elaborate frills at his wrist, and beneath his knee-breeches his stockings were canary yellow.

'Eleanor!' He flung his arms round her. 'This is a piece of good luck, seeing you here!'

Eleanor responded in kind. It would have been useless to expect Thomas to content himself with a simple, 'How do you do?' His artistic temperament demanded drama, and she knew from long experience that it had to be satisfied.

'My dear, you look wonderful. That pelisse —it must have come from the gods!'

'From Milsom Street, actually,' she teased him.

He looked at her reprovingly. 'You should not joke about such things. But I forgive you. Indeed, it would be churlish of me not to, after everything you have done for me. I am so glad I have seen you. I have wanted to speak to you ever since I heard! I've been meaning to thank you for all you have done.'

'Ah.' Eleanor paused. 'Arabella told you.'

'Of course she told me. And so she should have done. I cannot bear to think of what you

185

went through for my sake, and that of your dear sister. Having to speak to a *blackmailer* . . .' He pulled a silk handkerchief out of his coat-pocket and wafted it in front of his nose. 'It must have been too dreadful for words.' He shook his handkerchief out and put it carefully away. 'If only I'd known, I'd have gone to see the villain myself.'

Eleanor suppressed a sigh at the thought of Thomas visiting Mr Kendrick. If he had found Mr Kendrick alive it would have been bad enough, but his delicate temperament would never have coped with finding Mr Kendrick dead. However, Thomas did not know the full facts of the case, and Eleanor had no intention of revealing them.

'I never imagined you would do so in my stead.'

'You were in Cornwall at the time,' Eleanor reminded him practically, 'gathering fresh inspiration for your poetry.'

'Alas, yes. But to think of you in danger . . . I might be a poet, but I am still a man, and it was a man's mission.'

Eleanor's mouth quirked: Thomas was a dear boy, but he was really rather ridiculous! 'Calm yourself,' she said. 'I came to no harm.'

'It was very brave of you. But rest assured, you will never be plunged into such peril again. Arabella has destroyed the letters.'

Eleanor nodded. 'Yes, she told me. I think it was for the best.'

'Alas, those letters!' continued Thomas. 'So beautiful. But so indiscreet. We were both so young, I a mere stripling at university, and your beautiful sister still in the schoolroom. But when Cupid strikes, he does so without thought of age or reason. He simply fits his arrows and lets them fly!' He struck a dramatic pose. 'Still, all's well that ends well,' he said. He gave a sigh. 'It was a beautiful dream, but your sister has awoken and chosen her life-long swain.'

Eleanor patted his hand. 'I'm sure you will find a life-long love of your own,' she consoled him.

'Alas, I fear I am wedded to poetry and will never make any mortal woman my bride.'

This outrageous sentence was delivered with such a languorous look that Eleanor was tempted to laugh. However, to spare his feelings, she changed her laugh into a spluttering cough.

'But now, I must keep you no longer,' he said. 'I must away, for I have a poem to write which will not wait.'

And making her an extravagant bow he went on his way.

Eleanor laughed as she watched him go. Poor, dear Thomas! What ever could Arabella have seen in him? Still, at least Arabella had learnt the error of her ways. Charles would make her a far better husband.

She resettled her bonnet, which had almost

been tugged off in the breeze, and then set off for the circulating library.

*   *   *

Lucien prowled round the room he had hired at the local inn, glowering at the clock. It was still too early to go and see Eleanor. He had been determined not to speak to her until he had tied up all the loose ends of the Kendrick affair, but after seeing her at the ball he had decided he could wait no longer. He must speak to her and make her his. Growing tired of waiting, he took up his hat and set out for her house.

His way took him through the centre of Bath. He passed the elegant shops and the colourful parks . . . and then he saw Eleanor. Fortune had favoured him. She was just turning into Sidney Gardens.

He followed her, and had almost caught up with her when he saw something that shocked him so badly it made him stand stock still. She was greeting a young man . . . he was throwing his arms around her . . . and she was returning his embrace.

A few months ago he would not have believed it possible that seeing a young woman—any young woman—in the arms of another man could have given him such feelings of anger, pain, envy and despair, but those were the new and disturbing feelings that were suddenly warring in his breast.

Was it only last night he had danced with her? Spoken with her? And come to believe that his feelings were returned?

But now, with a sinking feeling, he saw the whole matter in a different light. What was it she had said? It began to come back to him. When he had said, 'You should have someone to take care of you,' she had said that she did not need anyone; that she had enough spirit to look after herself. And then, when he had called her Eleanor, she had protested, saying, 'It will arouse—*expectations*,' he had finished.

He had thought at the time it was simply maidenly modesty prompting her protest, but as a cold feeling invaded the pit of his stomach he feared he had been blind. It had not been expectations in herself that she had been implying. It must have been expectations in him. If they had not been interrupted, he feared she would have said that he must not raise his hopes; that he must not have any expectations; because she was in love with someone else.

No. He did not believe it. Her response to his kisses a few weeks before had been too ardent to be denied.

But was that not the problem? It had been a few weeks before. At which time he had not spoken. He had simply sent her home whilst he had sorted out the mess left by Kendrick's treachery and death. And in the meantime . . .

in the meantime she had met the young man he had seen her embracing in the Gardens.

His blood churned as he thought of it. The scene he had unwillingly witnessed had wrung his emotions, and filled him with unaccustomed pain. Eleanor—his Eleanor—had had an assignation. She had gone into Bath to meet a man—a fop! he thought in despair—and had then embraced the fool. He could not bear to think of it.

If only there could have been some mistake. But the gentleman had thrown his arms around her and she had not resisted. Instead, she had returned his embrace. And she had done it in a public place. How far must her feelings have gone for that to have happened? Far indeed.

He could not believe it. How could she want a dandified jackanapes? She had far too much spirit for that. Yet what else could he think?

'Lucien!'

He turned his head to see Charles at the other side of the road.

He quickly turned away again. He must not let Charles see him like this. He was aware of the fact that his face showed clearly what he was feeling, and he was glad that a steady stream of carriages prevented Charles from crossing the road straight away. It gave him time to school his features.

When he had done so, he turned towards Charles again.

'Well met!' said Charles companionably.

He made no mention of Lucien's expression, and Lucien was relieved to know that he had hidden his feelings well.

'You must be on your way to see Miss Grantham,' said Charles. 'I thought you weren't going until this afternoon. I'm just on my way to call on Arabella. We can go together.'

The last thing Lucien wanted to do was to visit the Granthams now, but he could not well refuse, and at least if he went this morning with Charles it would spare him the necessity of calling by himself in the afternoon, as he was engaged to do. That would be a torment he could not endure. And so, gritting his teeth, he fell into step beside Charles.

*   *   *

'I missed them?' Eleanor tried to keep the disappointment out of her voice when she returned home a short time later.

'Yes. They did not stay long, and have only just left. I invited Lord Silverton to call back later, but he said that unfortunately he had urgent business and would not be able to do so.'

'Oh. Never mind,' said Eleanor. She tried to sound unconcerned, but her disappointment showed.

'Why, Eleanor, I do believe he means

something to you.' Arabella looked at her searchingly. 'Are you in love with him?'

'Hush,' said Eleanor, flushing even more. 'Of course not.'

'He was remarkably handsome,' said Arabella innocently. 'And he seemed very taken with you. Especially on such a short acquaintance.'

'We had actually met before,' confessed Eleanor.

'Oh?' Arabella was surprised.

'Yes. At Lydia and Frederick's. You remember I told you I stayed with them for a night when I followed Mr Kendrick to London?'

'Of course. And Lord Silverton was there?'

Eleanor nodded.

'So that is why you were startled when Charles said he might be coming to the wedding. Oh, Eleanor, I do hope—'

'Now, Bella. You must not refine too much upon it,' said Eleanor hastily. She was not sure of Lucien's feelings, and until she was, she did not want to discuss it. 'Lord Silverton paid a call, that is all.'

'Of course. But all the same,' Arabella said impishly, 'you are not to get married until I return from the Lakes!'

CHAPTER EIGHT

Eleanor's eyes glowed with pride as she helped Arabella put the finishing touches to her wedding attire the following day.

'You look lovely, Bella,' she said.

'Are you sure my hair's all right?' asked Arabella nervously.

'It looks delightful,' Eleanor reassured her.

'You don't think Monsieur Legrand cut it too short?'

'No, it's beautiful,' said Eleanor, kissing her sister on the cheek. Her eyes misted. 'Mother and father would be so proud.'

'I'm glad.' Arabella stood back and surveyed Eleanor. 'And they would be proud of you.' She became more serious. 'I'm glad you have such a nice dress to wear. I know how hard it has been for you since our parents died, and how much you have sacrificed for me.'

'But not in vain!' remarked Eleanor.

Arabella dimpled. 'I know! I was so lucky to meet Charles. He is everything I've ever wanted from a man. He is handsome, charming, respectable and safe.'

There came the sound of carriages crunching on gravel below.

'Well, Bella, this is it,' said Eleanor.

Arabella nodded. Cheeks pink with excitement, she went out, with Eleanor close behind her. Lydia was sitting in one of the carriages with two little bridesmaids. She gave a cheery wave. She and Frederick had arrived in Bath the day before, in good time for the wedding. Arabella and Eleanor waved back, and then climbed into the front carriage with Frederick. Eleanor helped Arabella to arrange her dress so that the train would not crease, and then they were off.

The journey was slow and stately. On the way, Eleanor could not help her thoughts straying to Lucien. In only a little while she would see him again. Her heart warmed at the thought of it.

What did he have to say to her? she wondered. She did not know. But she knew what she wanted him to say . . .

At last the carriage pulled up outside the abbey. Arabella, looking radiant, alighted on the pavement, and Eleanor gave her sister her full attention. She arranged the folds of Arabella's beautiful white silk gown so that it draped elegantly around her slender figure, then Arabella took Frederick's arm, and Eleanor followed her sister into the abbey.

It was full to overflowing. The guest list was drawn from all the great and fashionable people of the moment, as well as family and friends of the bride and groom. As a future duke, Charles's wedding was one of note, and the *ton* had made an effort to attend. Dukes and duchesses, earls and countesses covered nearly every pew. Eleanor's eyes swept over them. There was Lord Accrington, with whom she had danced at the ball, and Lady Roskin, and . . . she frowned. Sitting in front of Lady Roskin was a gentleman she recognized but could not place. No matter. It was not important. Her eyes swept on. There was Sir Edward Makeroy, and Lord Stratton, but she could not see Lucien. She was disappointed, but reflected that with so many people in the abbey it was not to be wondered at, and besides, it was probably just as well, for if she had seen him she would have found it impossible to concentrate on her duties. And that was something she must do, for she did not want to let Arabella down.

She followed Arabella down the aisle, until at last she stood by the altar. She took her sister's bouquet and then melted into the background, leaving Arabella standing next to Charles, her starlike eyes turned trustingly to his. Charles was looking splendid. His clothes were an immaculate fit, and his fair hair was brushed into a fashionable Brutus hairstyle. But it was the look of love in his eyes that Eleanor admired more than all his style, for it was clear that he adored her sister. Arabella was destined to be a very happy woman.

There were a few last rustles, and one or two clearings of throats, and then a hush fell over the congregation.

'Dearly beloved . . .' The words of the

service resonated around the beautiful old abbey, and Eleanor gave herself up to an enjoyment of the service. Arabella rose to the occasion wonderfully, her vows ringing out in a clear tone, and Eleanor was so proud of her, for she knew how nervous she had been. The hymns, all specially chosen, were beautiful, and as the notes of the last one died away, Eleanor realized that her sister was now a married woman.

Arabella smiled adoringly at Charles, and then the organ struck up its joyful notes and the happy couple processed back down the aisle.

*   *   *

'Oh, Eleanor, I am having such a wonderful day!' said Arabella, once they arrived back at Ormston House after the ceremony. 'I was so nervous about the wedding, but do you know, it has been the best day of my life? And now I have the wedding breakfast to look forward to!'

Eleanor smiled to see Arabella's sparkling eyes. There was no doubt about it. Marriage suited her sister.

'I am so happy. I only wish you could be as happy, too. Perhaps Lord Silverton . . .'

Eleanor smiled. 'Now, Bella,' she said, 'I hope you are not turning into a matchmaker!'

'Well, you can't blame me for trying. I am so

happily married myself, that I would love to see you the same. Oh! Charles is calling me. I have to go and help him greet our guests.'

Eleanor went through into the drawing-room. She was the first to arrive, having travelled in the wedding procession, and for the moment the room was empty. It allowed her to see its full glory. The mirrors gleamed and the furniture shone. French doors led out on to the terrace. It looked inviting. The balustrade was topped with urns, and they were filled with flowers. Eleanor wandered out, enjoying their scent. Behind her, the drawing-room began to fill. The guests were arriving from the abbey and were milling about, exchanging greetings and remarking on the splendour of the wedding.

A breeze sprang up. It was cool, and Eleanor turned to go back inside. She went through the french doors, and then stopped as she saw Lucien. At that moment he turned and saw her. Her spirits lifted . . . and then fell. There was such a strange expression on his face that she felt suddenly cold. And then he turned away from her, and joined a small party by the window.

She felt as though she had received a physical blow. There had been something so remote about him. He had behaved like a total stranger. Why had he done it? She could not understand.

She thought back over the time she had

spent with him since he had arrived in Bath. Could he be angry that she had not been in when he had called upon her the previous day? Of course not. He had called before the appointed time, and besides, he was too reasonable to hold it against her that she had been out.

What then?

She thought back to their conversation at the ball, just before they had been interrupted. He had called her Eleanor, and she had told him he mustn't, because it would raise—

'Expectations?' he had queried.

She had not been going to say that. She had been going to say that it would raise eyebrows. But his immediate thought had been that it would raise expectations.

She felt a coldness in the pit of her stomach. Here, it seemed, was the answer to the mystery. He had withdrawn from her because he had realized that he had raised expectations that he had no intention of fulfilling.

She should have been pleased that he was not going to play with her affections, but instead she was devastated. It was an end to all her hopes. He did not love her. He did not want to make her his wife. And, so that there should be no further misunderstandings, he had behaved in a cool, if not to say ice-cold, way.

'Miss Grantham,' came a hail.

She turned towards Henry, the groomsman,

as he approached her, but she could not even force a smile.

'Why, Miss Grantham, you look very pale,' said Henry as he reached her side. 'Are you all right?'

'It is nothing,' she told him. 'The heat . . .'

'Yes, it is hot in here. The chandeliers give out more heat than you would imagine. And there are so many people. Would you like me to fetch you a glass of champagne?'

'Yes, please, if you would.'

She was glad of his absence, so that she had time to regain her composure. No matter how hurt she might be, she must not let it show. She did not want to arouse curiosity or, even worse, speculation. She must behave as though nothing untoward had happened.

Even so, she was devastated.

Henry soon returned, and she sipped her champagne.

'Better?' he asked her hopefully.

'Yes, thank you. Much better,' she said.

But she was not. Across the room, Lucien was offering his arm to a pretty young blonde and escorting her into the dining-room.

She must not think of it. He had made it clear that, whatever their relationship might have been in the past, it was now to be nothing more than a slight acquaintance. It was small consolation to tell herself that he had retreated for honourable reasons; that, realizing he had aroused her expectations, he had withdrawn, so as not to occasion further pain. But the fact remained that he *had* withdrawn from her and it had left a gaping hole at the heart of her.

'Here, take my arm,' said Henry chivalrously. 'I am to take you in.'

Eleanor put her empty champagne-glass on the tray of a passing footman, and then taking Henry's arm she went into the dining-room. It looked magnificent. Snowy cloths covered the tables, which sparkled with silver cutlery and the finest crystal. Huge pyramids of fruit were arranged as centrepieces. Flowers were festooned around the ceiling, and hung in dazzling streamers down the walls. If Eleanor had not felt so desolate she would have exclaimed how charming it was.

The wedding breakfast began. All manner of tempting delicacies were spread out on the snowy white cloths as one course succeeded another. Oyster patties, turbot set in smelts, venison and partridges à la Pompadour paraded across the cloths. The sparkling glasses were filled with the finest wines, and footmen walked round with trays of champagne. It should have raised her spirits. But instead, Eleanor's heart sank. Wonderful though the food was, she could not eat any of it. After all that had happened, she had completely lost her appetite. But she must make at least a show of eating. Slowly, mechanically, she took a mouthful of oyster patty and did her best to eat it.

The meal seemed endless. Cold meats, pheasant pie, fruit tarts and syllabubs passed by, whilst all around her the other guests were laughing, eating, chattering and enjoying themselves. She did her best to make conversation with Henry, and with Sir William Pondersny, who sat on her other side. She talked about the splendour of the arrangements and the wonderful food, but it was only when talking about Arabella, and how beautiful she had looked as a bride that she was able to muster any genuine animation.

At last the meal was over. Even the most voracious of guests had eaten their fill. It was time to return to the drawing-room. A small orchestra was beginning to play.

'I didn't think we'd see Silverton here today,' said Henry as they rose from the table.

At this unexpected mention of Lucien, Eleanor looked instinctively towards him . . . to find that his eyes were fixed on her. There was such a peculiar expression in them, of pain and longing, that her heart turned over inside her.

But before she could wonder what his expression might mean, she saw a gentleman walk over to him and engage him in conversation. Her attention was caught. It was the gentleman she had recognized in the abbey.

Now where have I seen him before? thought

Eleanor. For she was sure she *had* seen the gentleman somewhere before.

But no. It was no good. She could not place him.

Lucien left the dining-room. The gentleman went with him, and she followed on Henry's arm.

And then she suddenly froze, for she had just remembered where she had seen Lucien's companion, and it made her blood run cold.

As she entered the drawing-room she saw the gentleman leave, and knew that she must speak to Lucien at once. Despite his coldness, this was a matter of such urgency that she had to seek him out, even if it meant risking a second rebuff.

Excusing herself from Henry, she went over to him.

'Lord Silverton,' she said.

His back was towards her, and he did not at once turn round. For a moment she thought he would ignore her. But then, slowly, he turned. 'Miss Grantham.'

His manner was still cold, but his eyes . . . she could not allow herself to think about his eyes.

'I must speak to you on a matter of urgency,' she said.

He looked as though he was about to refuse, but she could not allow him to do so.

'The gentleman you were with . . .' she said hurriedly.

At her words, his expression changed. He became more alert. 'Drayforth?' he asked.

She nodded. 'I have seen him before.'

'Very possibly. He came to my house in London, if you remember.'

She shook her head. 'No. It wasn't there.'

Before she could say any more the musicians finished playing, and there was a lull in the general conversation. She could not go on without being overheard.

'I must speak to you at once, in private,' she said in a low voice. 'Meet me in the conservatory.'

She knew the house well. The conservatory would give them the privacy they needed.

Without waiting for him to reply she hurried out of the dining-room. Once she reached the conservatory she went inside. It was almost like a jungle, so full was it of lush and exotic plants. They filled every available space, shielding the discreetly placed chairs. It was here that Charles had proposed to Arabella, in a private nook. But today it must serve a different purpose.

She paced to and fro in a small, secluded corner as her busy mind turned over all the implications of what she had just discovered.

A few minutes later Lucien joined her.

How distant he looked. But she had something of such importance to communicate that she must put everything else out of her mind.

'You wanted to speak to me?' he asked.

Despite her good intentions, their lack of rapport hurt her.

She mastered her emotions. 'It's about Drayforth,' she said.

'Go on.'

'I've just remembered where I've seen him before. It was in the yard of the coaching inn, in Bath, many weeks ago, just before you held up the stagecoach. I had been to see Mr Kendrick and found him not at home, so I went to the inn intending to buy a cup of chocolate whilst I thought over what to do. I saw Mr Kendrick standing in the coaching yard, talking to another gentleman.' She looked him in the eye. 'That other gentleman was Drayforth.'

Lucien turned pale. 'You're saying that Drayforth knew Kendrick?'

Eleanor nodded.

Lucien's face became grim. 'So that's it. We'd suspected for some time that Kendrick might have had inside help. He seemed to steal all the most important papers, and to know exactly where they were. But I never suspected Drayforth. Although I should have guessed. That night—the night I was overcome by gas,' he explained. 'The night you saved me.'

His voice softened, and for a moment she remembered how close they had been that night at Silverton House. There was a warmth

204

in his glance that told her he was remembering it, too. There had been a connection between them then. The evening had been magical, with laughter and friendship, and they had discovered they had a strong rapport. They had learnt about each other's lives, and what they had learnt had brought them closer. And then had come the night. When Lucien had been overcome by the gas Eleanor's emotions had intensified. And so, she had thought, had his. The way he had touched her when she had said she must retire for the night had made her heart sing. She could still remember it, the way her skin had tingled at his touch. And she would never forget his kiss. It had been utterly mesmerizing. She had wanted him to kiss her and kiss her and never stop. And when he had finally let her go, she had been filled with an insane longing to initiate a kiss herself. It had been unmaidenly, she knew, but the feel of his lips on hers had been so wonderful that she had wanted to experience it again. To her chagrin, she realized she wanted to experience it now. Against all reason she wanted him to take her into his arms and kiss her on the lips, softly and tenderly, or hard and passionately, for each way was as wonderful as the other.

He seemed to sense something of her feelings, and the atmosphere became charged. For a minute she thought he was actually going to do it. His head bent towards her. But then his expression changed.

He has remembered something, she thought. He has remembered that he must not raise my expectations. Her heart sank. But she could do nothing about it. It was useless to tell herself that if Lucien did not love her, that she should not want him to touch her, for she did. But he was not going to do it. And even if he did, she would push him away. Her pride, her self-respect, would demand it.

Gaining some semblance of control, she brought her thoughts back to the present.

He, too, had recovered himself. His softer expression vanished, and he became distant once more.

'Drayforth was in the house that night,' he said, 'but once I had recovered from my brush with death, I didn't suspect him of being involved. I should have done. I was suspicious of the accident. It seemed too much of a coincidence that it should happen on the very night I had important documents in the house. I was also suspicious of the fact that the gas had rendered me unconscious before I had noticed the lights blowing out.'

'You said that it must have been because you had fallen asleep before it happened,' Eleanor reminded him.

She saw his expression, and realization dawned on her.

'You never believed that,' she said. 'You simply said it to reassure me.'

'There was no point in worrying you. But

206

still, I almost came to believe it myself. When no forced entry could be found, and when I realized that the documents had not been taken, I thought it must have been an accident after all.'

'But it was Drayforth,' said Eleanor.

'Yes. He was alone in the dining-room for a few minutes whilst Beddows announced him. He must have tampered with the port,' said Lucien grimly.

'So you didn't fall asleep. You were drugged,' said Eleanor, understanding.

'Exactly. It was lucky for me I took only one glass. If I had been a heavy drinker, like Drayforth, I would have had three or four, and it would have taken me a lot longer to throw off the effects. He must have been expecting that, or he would have put a greater concentration of the drug in the decanter.'

'And then, when you were asleep, he broke in and blew out the gas.'

'He did not need to break in. After our conversation he said he would show himself out. I let him. He had been to the house a number of times before and he knew the way and so I saw no reason to go with him.'

'But he never left. He must have been there all the time,' said Eleanor, 'waiting for you to drink the port.'

'And once he'd given the drug time to take effect he walked into the dining-room and blew out the gas.'

Eleanor shuddered at the thought of it.

'It was very neat,' went on Lucien. 'If you hadn't found me, I would have been killed, and my death would have been put down to a tragic accident. He would never have been suspected.'

'Not even when the documents were found to have been missing? That was his motive, wasn't it? He wanted to steal the documents back again.'

'He did. He knew it would not seem suspicious if they could not be found after my death, because he was the only person who was aware I'd managed to retrieve them. If they had not been there when my effects had been examined, it would simply have been assumed that I had failed in my endeavours to get them back from Kendrick.'

'And did he manage to steal them?' asked Eleanor.

'No. But if you had not come downstairs when you did, he would have done. Your appearance forced him to leave the house. You foiled his plan in more ways than one.'

He gave her a tender look. But then his expression became remote and he continued.

'Now I know why Kendrick's case was empty when I held up the stagecoach. Drayforth must have been warning Kendrick about what was going to happen when you saw them at the inn. Kendrick must have slipped the papers into his pocket.'

'It must have been a lucrative partnership,' said Eleanor.

Lucien agreed. 'Drayforth would know which papers to take, and where they could be found, and then Kendrick would steal them before selling them on. I have to get this information to the right ears. Fortunately there are some very influential people here today and I won't have far to go. But I'm not leaving you alone until Drayforth's been picked up. If he guesses that you've recognized him, then you'll be in danger.'

He took her hand. Foolish though it was, she revelled in the touch of his strong, firm fingers. His eyes met hers.

Then, as if remembering the urgency of the situation, he offered her his arm. 'We must hurry,' he said, and led her towards the drawing-room. He dropped her hand as they entered, but kept so close to her that the tails of his coat brushed the skirt of her gown.

Standing at the side of the room was an elderly man in military uniform. It was towards him that Lucien headed.

He spoke in a low voice. 'A word, sir.'

The older man turned towards him with a bland expression. Anyone watching them would think they were talking of nothing more alarming than the splendour of the wedding or the beauty of the bride. But Eleanor could tell by the shrewd light in the older man's eye that Lucien had his full attention.

Smiling all the while, to accentuate the impression that they were talking of the wedding, Lucien explained the situation. The older man's expression remained bland, but once Lucien had finished he declared his intention of going home.

'Good to see you Silverton. I'm glad you're enjoying the celebrations, but I find them rather tiring. I'm not as young as I used to be, alas,' he said, in a voice loud enough for those around him to overhear. 'I fear I must find our hostess and excuse myself. We old men need to take care of ourselves.'

He bowed to those around him, and could be seen taking his leave of his hosts a few minutes later.

'There's no more to be done for the present,' said Lucien, as the elderly gentleman walked out of the room. 'The general will set things in motion, and before the evening's over Drayforth will have been picked up. It's a good thing Cooper's still with you. You will need someone to watch over you for the next few months. Drayforth will have associates, and if he remembers seeing you at the coaching inn he will realize how his treachery was discovered, and you will not be safe.' He paused. 'Eleanor . . .'

There was something in his tone that caught her attention. 'Yes?' she asked gently, when he did not continue.

His tone, too, had gentled. He appeared to

be wrestling with himself. There was something he wanted to say, it seemed, but he did not know how to say it. 'Eleanor, when I came to call on you—that is, yesterday . . .' He tried again. 'Eleanor, when I saw . . .'

Then, seeming to come to a sudden resolution, he looked her in the eyes.

'Eleanor, I need to know whether—'

'Eleanor! There you are!'

Lydia's happy voice broke in on them.

Lucien cursed under his breath, and Eleanor tried to swallow her disappointment and frustration. She had the feeling he had been about to explain why he had been so distant and cold. Although perhaps it was better not to hear it. To have him put it into words; to hear him say, 'Eleanor, I'm sorry if I gave you a false impression, but I don't love you,' would have been just too terrible.

But now Lydia and Frederick had joined them, and he would have no chance to say anything further.

'Isn't this the most wonderful wedding!' sighed Lydia. 'Arabella looks like a dream. And Charles looks so handsome. It is the best wedding I can ever remember—apart from my children's and my own, that is!'

'I'm glad to see you here, Silverton,' said Frederick. 'The last time we met you didn't think you were going to be able to come.'

The gentlemen were soon deep in conversation, and Lydia drew Eleanor a little aside.

'My dear Eleanor, I know it's none of my business, but as your mother is no longer alive I am sure you will not mind if I give you a word of advice.' She hesitated, and then said in a rush, 'I don't like to think of you making an assignation with a man like that.'

Eleanor's spirits sank. Evidently Lydia had seen her going into the conservatory, and had seen Lucien going in a few minutes after her.

'Oh, I know what you're going to say,' went on Lydia. 'He's from a good family. And it's true. But all the same, I shouldn't like a daughter of mine getting mixed up with him.'

'I know Lord Silverton has a wild reputation,' said Eleanor, wondering how much she should say, 'but—'

'Lucien?' Lydia looked surprised. 'No, I don't mean Lucien. He might be wild, but underneath he's an honourable man. No, it's not Lucien I'm talking about.' She hesitated. 'I wanted to find you earlier. I was going to invite you to spend a few weeks with Frederick and myself when Arabella went off on her honeymoon. We have a mind to make a tour of Derbyshire, and we thought you might like to join us. I saw you slipping into the conservatory. There's no need to worry,' she hurried on, 'I won't say anything to anyone. But I have heard things about him that make me concerned. When Caroline, my youngest daughter, had her come-out I learnt all about

212

the eligible young men who attended the Season's entertainments, and the things I heard about him made me want to keep Caroline away from him. I know I shouldn't interfere but . . . well, my dear, I should be happier if you did not see him again.'

Eleanor was having difficulty following the thread of Lydia's conversation.

'The man I met in the conservatory?'

'That's right,' Lydia nodded.

'Who is not Lord Silverton?'

'No.'

'But I didn't meet anyone in the conservatory,' she said.

'So you didn't meet Mr Drayforth?' Lydia gave a sigh of relief. 'Forgive me, my dear. I have been jumping to conclusions. But when I saw him watching you, and then I saw him slipping into the conservatory, with you following him a minute or two later, I naturally assumed—'

'Drayforth?' Eleanor's stomach lurched and she felt a sudden ringing in her ears.

'Yes. I thought you'd gone to see him.'

'You mean Mr Drayforth was in the conservatory?' she asked in a whisper.

'Yes. Didn't you see him?'

'No.'

Eleanor thought of all the greenery in the conservatory, where the citrus trees and the potted plants obscured carefully placed seats and secret corners. If Mr Drayforth had been in the conservatory when she had entered it then he had heard everything she had said to Lucien.

'My dear, are you all right?' asked Lydia in concern. 'You've gone very pale.'

'No, I feel a little faint.'

Eleanor's eyes went to Lucien. He and Frederick had walked across the room in search of a glass of champagne.

'I think if we could rejoin the gentlemen . . .' said Eleanor.

'Of course, my dear. One of them can find you a seat.'

The two ladies set off across the room, but just as Eleanor thought they were going to be able to reach the gentlemen, strong hands seized her from behind and thrust her to the side. She tried to twist out of her abductor's hands, but she was held in a vicelike grip.

Thwarted in this, she opened her mouth to call for help, but a hissing voice said, 'I shouldn't do that, if I were you. Your lady friend's perfectly safe at the moment. She thinks she was separated from you in the crush. Look, she's over there, trying to find you.'

Eleanor saw that such was the case. Lydia was turning round, looking bewildered, not far away.

'Do you see that man behind her?'

Eleanor saw a tall man dogging Lydia's footsteps.

'As long as you co-operate he will do nothing. But one sound from you and it'll be the worse for her.'

Before Eleanor could think of a way out of her predicament, much less act, she was pushed out of the drawing-room, along the landing and into a small ante-room. It was dark. Only the glow coming from the fire illuminated it. A figure detached itself from the shadows and in the flickering light of the flames Eleanor recognized Mr Drayforth. He lit the candles that stood on the mantelpiece and then turned to face her. 'So, Miss Grantham, it seems you recognized me at the coaching inn,' he said. 'A pity.' He took her chin between his fingers and turned her face to his. Eleanor, her arms held behind her back, wrenched her face away. Drayforth laughed softly.

'I suggest you let me go,' she said. 'I was seen leaving the drawing-room. When Lucien gets here—'

'Ah, yes, your protector. Lord Silverton. Pardon me for mentioning it, Miss Grantham, but he is not a wise choice for a spinster lady to fix on. Lucien is definitely not the marrying kind. You would have done better to develop a *tendre* for one of the other gentlemen here tonight. Although now, of course, it no longer matters. You have endangered my safety, and no matter how much it pains me to say it, I am going to have to—'

215

He broke off as the door opened and Eleanor's spirits soared. There, framed in the doorway, was Lucien.

She was just about to make a bid for freedom, using his entrance as a distraction, when she suddenly froze. For behind Lucien was another man. And he was holding a pistol to Lucien's head.

Drayforth spoke mockingly. 'My dear Silverton, do come in.'

'Drayforth.' There was a note of steel in Lucien's voice. He might be in an unenviable position at the moment, but Eleanor could tell from his tone of voice that he had not given up, and that he meant to change the situation as soon as an opportunity presented itself.

'How kind of you to join us. Miss Grantham and I were just having a little tête-à-tête. But I'm sure we will enjoy it even more if you join us.'

The man behind Lucien gave a sneer and pushed him roughly into the room.

'What are we going to do with them?' he demanded.

'You will have to forgive him,' said Drayforth apologetically. 'Hoskins has no finesse.'

The man called Hoskins snorted.

'As to what we're going to do with them,' said Drayforth, now addressing Hoskins, 'that is something I haven't yet quite decided. But whatever it is, we won't be doing it here. At

216

least, not anything permanent. There's too much chance of our being discovered.'

Hoskins nodded. Then raising his pistol, he brought it down with a crack on Lucien's head.

'No!' Eleanor struggled to break free as Lucien crumpled to the floor, but strong hands held her and she could not go to him.

And then she felt a blow to her own head, and everything went black.

*   *   *

Drayforth looked down at the two bodies that lay at his feet.

'Now what?' Hoskins spoke brusquely.

'Now we get them away from here,' Drayforth said.

'And take them to the town house?'

'No. I don't want them anywhere near the general.' He looked at Hoskins. 'You've taken care of him?'

Hoskins nodded. 'I followed him out of the house and bundled him into a hackney carriage, just like you said. He won't be telling anyone about what he's learnt.'

'Good.' Drayforth turned back to Lucien and Eleanor, who lay unconscious on the floor. 'Silverton will be useful. He knows a great many things.'

'And the girl?'

'She, too, will be useful. We can use her as a lever to make him talk. We'll take them to my estate. That way, we can hold them indefinitely with no one being any the wiser.'

'There'll be a hue and cry,' objected Hoskins.

'I don't think so. I have an idea of how to avoid it.' He looked at Hoskins. 'Have the carriage taken round to the mews, then take these two out the back way. Make sure you're not seen. I will join you there when I've carried out my plan.'

Hoskins nodded, and lifted Eleanor's unconscious form.

The two ruffians by the door lifted Lucien between them, and once they had departed, Drayforth returned to the ballroom.

*   *   *

'Have you seen Eleanor?' Lydia asked anxiously as she joined Arabella at the side of the ballroom. 'I was talking to her just now but she felt faint. Somehow we got separated and I'm worried about her. I hope she's all right.'

'No,' said Arabella. 'I didn't know she was feeling ill.'

'It came over her suddenly. I dare say it was the heat.'

At that moment Charles came up.

'What is it?' he asked, as he saw Arabella's worried face.

'Lydia was talking to Eleanor just now, but she felt unwell and so they went in search of

218

Frederick. But Lydia became separated from her and she hasn't been able to find her again.'

'If Eleanor was feeling faint, perhaps she went into one of the ante-rooms,' said Charles practically. 'It's a lot cooler in there. I'll send one of the footmen to look for her.' He looked round, preparing to call one of the footmen.

Mr Drayforth, who had drawn closer, caught his eye.

'Yes?' asked Charles.

Mr Drayforth hesitated, apparently loath to say what must be said.

'Have you seen her?' asked Arabella. 'Is she all right?'

By this time the people standing nearby had stopped what they were doing and were listening curiously to the tense exchange.

'I'm sorry to be the bearer of bad news,' said Mr Drayforth. He hesitated, then went on with apparent reluctance. 'The thing is, I overheard your sister talking to Lord Silverton in the conservatory earlier this evening. I did not mean to listen, but they had obviously not seen me as I was obscured by a particularly large plant, and when I was about to reveal myself I heard a host of endearments and stayed where I was—I did not want to cause embarrassment.'

'Thank you,' said Charles coldly.

'They were discussing their plans for a journey,' continued Mr Drayforth. 'I did not like to speculate as to the nature of the journey at the time, it being none of my business, but under the circumstances I feel I must speak. I am afraid they have run away together.'

There was a stunned silence. And then the whispers began, running round the room as the rumour spread like wildfire.

'Run away?' asked Arabella, looking distinctly pale.

'I'm afraid so. Unless they want to be found, I don't believe we will see them again.'

The whispers were becoming louder.

Charles, regaining his wits, rose to the occasion. Speaking loudly enough for everyone to hear, he said to Arabella, 'Come, my love. Do not distress yourself: this is all hearsay. You and I know that Eleanor would never run off with anyone, least of all Lord Silverton. As for this gentleman,' he said, turning his head slightly towards Mr Drayforth, 'I'm sure he is speaking the truth as he knows it, but *eavesdroppers*'—he lingered on the word, to make it quite clear what he thought of Mr Drayforth—'are prone to misunderstandings. Eleanor was feeling unwell, you say. Then it is my belief she has gone no further than the ladies' withdrawing room. In fact, it would not surprise me if that is the "journey" Mr Drayforth overheard them discussing. Eleanor, no doubt, was expressing her desire to retire and Lord Silverton, as a gentleman, offered to escort her. I will send one of the servants to enquire after your sister's health.'

'Leave it to me,' said Lydia, who had been hovering nearby.

'Thank you,' said Charles.

Then he turned back to Arabella. 'In the meantime, my love, there is someone I am longing for you to meet.'

Arabella, strengthened by Charles's expert handling of the situation, took her lead from him, and with surprising assurance she took his hand. 'Of course, Eleanor must have gone to the ladies' withdrawing room,' she said calmly. 'Mr Drayforth must have misheard. As you say, eavesdroppers rarely hear the truth.'

And with a contemptuous look at Mr Drayforth, she swept past him on Charles's arm.

'Well done, my love,' said Charles to Arabella.

'Oh, Charles, I never thought I would be able to do such a thing. But once you stood up to that terrible man I knew I must do the same. Even so, I would not have managed it if you had not been by my side.'

Charles gave her hand an affectionate squeeze.

'But I am worried. What did he mean by inventing such a monstrous thing?' Her voice wavered. 'He did invent it, didn't he? You don't think Eleanor and Lord Silverton—'

'I think we should wait and see if Eleanor is here.'

'And if Lord Silverton is still here?'

Charles called over a passing footman and gave him instructions to find Lord Silverton.

'But Charles, what if they really have run off together? Eleanor was talking to Lord Silverton this afternoon. I don't think she would do such a thing, but perhaps . . . he is so very handsome . . . and I think Eleanor has feelings for him.'

'The most important thing is for us to act as though nothing untoward has happened,' said Charles, giving Arabella's arm another squeeze. 'That way, our guests will decide it is all a hum and the gossip will die down.'

'And if it isn't a hum?' asked Arabella, worried.

His hand tightened over hers. 'Eleanor is over age. She is old enough to make her own decisions. If she has really run off with Lord Silverton, my love, then I am afraid there is nothing we can do about it.'

CHAPTER NINE

Eleanor felt a rolling movement beneath her as she slowly came to her senses. Her head was throbbing. She felt sick, and she could not remember who she was or where she was. But gradually she began to recover her memories. She had been knocked unconscious by Mr Drayforth's cronies, and evidently she was now in a carriage. Cautiously opening her eyes a fraction, she was frustrated to discover that she had been thrown down with her face pressed against the squabs. She could see very little. But the squabs were upholstered in velvet, so it was not a hackney carriage, and its owner must be rich.

It was Mr Drayforth's carriage, then, she reasoned. And she was being taken—where?

She would soon know for certain. The carriage was beginning to slow, and at last it rolled to a halt. Closing her eyes firmly she went limp, so that when she was seized by rough hands, she appeared to be still unconscious. She was slung unceremoniously over someone's shoulder, and risked opening her eyes a fraction again as she was carried forward.

She could see a road beneath her, but it was a rough, narrow one, and she guessed they were not in London.

Did Mr Drayforth have an estate? she wondered. If so, that was where she guessed they were. But it could not be too far from Bath. The night was not yet dark, so they could not be more than a few hours' drive away.

The rough road beneath her gave way to a threshold, and she was carried into a mean dwelling with a rush-strewn floor. She was taken through one large room and into a second, smaller room that led off it.

She was thrown into a corner, on to a dirty

pallet, and left there. Again she could see nothing. Her face was to the wall, and she dare not change her position for fear of drawing attention to herself. But she could hear voices.

'Where shall I put him?' came a rough voice.

'Over here. Tie him to the chair.'

There was the sound of a body being set down, and ropes being tied. Her spirits lifted. If he was being tied, then Lucien must still be alive. But then they fell again. He might be alive, but he was bound, and so was she.

'What do we do now?' came the rough voice again.

'We wait for Drayforth. He'll want to question them when he gets here. I'm going up to the house. There are some things he wants me to get ready for him. You're to stay here and keep watch.'

There was the sound of two sets of footsteps walking out of the room. That was lucky. The ruffian who was to guard them was not going to remain in the same room. She did not know what she could do, but at least if she was not closely watched there was a chance she could do something.

She waited until the footsteps had stopped, one set going out of the cottage and the other stopping in the next room.

Then cautiously she tried to stand up. It was difficult with her hands tied, but at last she managed it. Then she went over to Lucien.

She knelt down in front of him . . . and his eyes opened. 'Lucien!' she said. 'You're alive. Thank God!'

'And you.' His eyes were warm, and she felt a surge in her spirits. But there was no time for anything further. They must use the time they had alone to plan their escape.

'I think we're at Drayforth's country estate,' she whispered. 'I came to my senses before I was carried into the cottage, and managed to see something of our surroundings,' she explained.

He nodded. 'I think you're right. His estate is not far from Bath, and he would find it the most convenient place to bring us, particularly at such short notice. This is probably one of the labourers' cottages.'

'He's not much of a landlord,' said Eleanor, looking round the cottage. The walls were uneven, and the floor was made of mud, over which were scattered dirty rushes.

'I agree,' said Lucien with a wry smile. 'But we have more important things to think about. Such as getting out of here before Drayforth returns. Until then we're safe. His henchmen won't do anything without him.'

'I'm surprised he's not here already,' said Eleanor.

'He would not want to attract attention by leaving the celebrations early. He would want to behave like any other guest. I only hope he didn't get to the general.'

'The man you set on his trail?' asked Eleanor.

Lucien nodded. 'Still, we can't worry about that now.'

'No. We have other things to worry about.'

Eleanor strained at the ropes which bound her wrists, but it was no good, they were too firmly tied for her to be able to get free. And Lucien was in an even worse predicament. By the dim light of the moon drifting in through the high, narrow window she could see that he was tied to a rickety chair. His legs were tied to the chair legs and his hands were tied behind him before being tied to the chair back.

'I can stand, but I certainly can't overpower our guard,' said Eleanor, 'and even if I could, you couldn't possibly walk like that.'

'I shouldn't need to,' he surprised her by saying, 'I have a knife in my pocket.'

Her eyebrows lifted.

'This kind of situation is not unknown to me,' he said with a wry smile. 'It's as well to be prepared.'

'Even when attending a wedding?'

'Traitors don't allow themselves to be sidetracked by considerations such as that.'

'No, I don't suppose they do,' she agreed. 'Which pocket is your knife in?'

'The right one.'

She looked doubtful. With her hands tied behind her back, getting the knife out of his pocket would not be easy. She said nothing of

226

her doubts to Lucien, however. Something must be done to save them, and this was the only chance they had.

She turned round slowly, so that her back was towards him. Then, edging backwards on her knees, she came to rest with her hands against his coat. She felt her way across his body until she found the hard ridge made by his knife. She managed to hook her fingers round the opening of his pocket and then sent them questing downwards, feeling for the hilt. She touched it, and wrapped her fingers round it, but she could not grip it sufficiently well to pull it out.

'I can't do it,' she said. 'The ropes are so tight they've cut off most of the circulation in my hands.'

'Yes, you can,' he said encouragingly. 'Rub your hands together to restore your circulation and try again.'

She did as he suggested, rubbing her hands awkwardly together, and managed to improve her circulation. Then, readjusting her position and rising a little higher on her knees, she tried again.

This time she managed to grasp the hilt firmly. But just as she was about to pull it out she hesitated.

'If I pull it out awkwardly, it will cut you,' she said.

'Don't worry. It's sheathed.'

Reassured, she wrapped her fingers firmly

around the knife and pulled hard. It moved.

'You're doing it,' he said.

She tugged on it again, and succeeded in drawing it out above the top of his pocket. But her hands were aching, and she stopped to rest them. She was just flexing her fingers when she heard the sound of horses approaching the cottage. Drayforth!

Spurred on, she seized the knife and managed to pull it free. But there was no time to cut Lucien's bonds.

'Get away,' he hissed, as voices approached the other side of the door.

She threw herself on to the pallet, mimicking her earlier position by throwing herself down with her face against the wall. The knife was in front of her, concealed in the folds of her skirt. She closed her eyes, feigning unconsciousness, and waited.

The door opened, and the light of a lantern spilled into the room.

From where she was lying she could not see what was happening, but she heard the sound of footsteps entering the room, and then Drayforth's voice said, 'Ah, Silverton. You've come round.'

'As you see.' Lucien's reply was bravely uttered, and anyone hearing him without seeing him would never have guessed that he was bound hand and foot.

'Good.'

'I see you've brought another couple of

ruffians with you,' said Lucien scathingly.

Eleanor's heart sank. How was she possibly to get away, and Lucien too, if Drayforth now had three accomplices?

Lucien's voice continued mockingly. 'I might have known you'd be unwilling to tackle a man who's bound hand and foot on your own.'

'Very amusing,' replied Drayforth.

His words were bland but his tone showed that Lucien's words had made him angry.

Eleanor heard two sets of footsteps taking a few paces, and realized that two of the men had taken up their places, one on either side of the door.

Her heart sank still further. But she must not give way. There was still a chance that she would be able to escape. She could not at present try to pull Lucien's knife out of its scabbard and cut her ropes, as any movement on her part would be seen. But perhaps, if they were left alone, she would be able to get free.

'Now, Lucien, it's time you and I had a little talk.'

'Yes, let's,' said Lucien.

Eleanor was amazed at how calm he sounded. Although she knew he was used to dangerous situations, he surely couldn't ever have been in a worse predicament than this.

'I'd be interested to know just when you decided to turn traitor,' Lucien continued.

'Traitor?' Drayforth sounded amused. 'I'm

not a traitor. I'm as loyal as I've ever been—to myself. My arrangement with Kendrick was very lucrative.' His voice became musing. 'It's a pity it had to end.'

Something in his tone alerted Eleanor, and a flash of understanding hit her. It was Drayforth who had killed Mr Kendrick.

The same flash of understanding had evidently hit Lucien at the same moment. 'It was you who killed him.'

'It was indeed. I didn't want to. He was still of use to me. But the highway robbery made him greedy. He was running risks, he said. He wanted a bigger share of the profits.'

'I should have guessed.'

'You would have done in time, which is why I tried to kill you, too. You were already beginning to suspect that Kendrick had a contact on the inside, and it wouldn't have been long before you'd started to suspect me. An accident with the gas—so unreliable, this new form of lighting—and you were no further threat. But it didn't quite work. Miss Grantham interrupted me and I had to flee. A pity. I hadn't had time to find the documents so I had to abandon them. But I didn't abandon my attempt to kill you. Sooner or later, you would have met with another accident. It's just that, when I overheard Miss Grantham in the conservatory and knew that she had recognized me, I realized it would have to be sooner.'

'So what is it going to be? A carriage accident? A pistol that blows up in my face? Whatever it is, questions will be asked.'

'I don't think so. You see, I have started a rumour that you have run away with Miss Grantham. So if you are never seen again no one will wonder at it. They will assume you are hiding out in Wales, or Scotland, or some other such remote place.'

'You did what?'

Drayforth smirked. 'You don't like the idea? I thought it was rather good. An accident is always a messy thing—as you say, there's always the possibility that someone will become suspicious and questions will be asked. But this way, no one will know you are dead. They will simply think you have chosen to disappear. No fuss, no mess, no problem.'

'You don't really think the general will let it rest at that?' demanded Lucien.

'The general has been taken care of,' remarked Drayforth drily.

There was a deathly silence.

Then Lucien, recovering himself, said, 'And what about Miss Grantham? She has powerful relatives. They won't believe a word of it.'

'You think not? I'm not so sure. Oh, they put a good face on it, of course. They declared it was nonsense, and said that Miss Grantham had simply retreated to her room with a bad head. But when she isn't seen, and you are also missing, the rumour will be believed, and no one will come looking for you.'

Eleanor felt her spirits sink. She had been hoping that Charles would have sent out footmen to look for her, but in the circumstances he wouldn't be doing any such thing. Their only hope now lay in Cooper. Knowing that she and Lucien had been involved in a dangerous enterprise, Eleanor hoped he would not believe Drayforth's lies and would see fit to investigate. But he was a man of action, not planning, and he would need help to set a rescue in motion. All of which would take time. So that if they wanted to escape, they would have to do it themselves.

'You—' began Lucien angrily.

'Careful, now. There's a lady present,' Drayforth taunted him. 'Although, unfortunately, not a conscious one. Never mind. Give her time. Now, I've answered your questions, so you can answer mine. I've a mind to know how many troops—'

'I'm not answering any of your questions,' growled Lucien.

'Do you know? I believe you. And even if I told my friends here to hit you, I don't think they'd be able to make you oblige. But if I get them to hit Miss Grantham once she's come round, I think you'll co-operate: it's one thing for you to remain silent when a fist is finding its way into your face, it's quite another when it's finding its way into Miss Grantham's.'

'You cur,' roared Lucien. There was a

232

scraping sound, and Eleanor realized that, despite being tied to a chair, Lucien was trying to throw himself at Drayforth.

'Not at all,' remarked Drayforth. 'Just a believer in free enterprise. I'll leave you to think about what I've said. Of course, if you co-operate, Miss Grantham needn't be hurt at all. It's your choice. I hope for her sake you make the right one.'

Eleanor heard the sound of footsteps, and knew that Drayforth was leaving the room. There was the sound of a bar being dropped on the other side of the door.

But what about the guards? Not for the first time, she wished she could see what was happening. Had Drayforth left the guards in the room? Or, it being so small, had he taken them through to the next room?

There was a silence.

Then Lucien whispered, 'Eleanor.'

'Yes?'

'They've gone.'

She gave a sigh of relief.

Outside the cottage, she could hear the sound of a horse snuffling, and then a minute later came the sound of hoofs. They gradually picked up speed and she guessed that Drayforth was riding away. A light from the next room, however, showed that he had not taken his henchmen with him. They had stayed behind, on guard.

There was no time to delay. The guards

233

could decide to come into the room at any time. Giving her attention to the business of cutting her ropes, she turned herself with difficulty on the dirty pallet until she could grasp the knife, then pulled it out of its sheath. She tried to rub the ropes over the blade, but to her frustration they just kept pushing the knife away. Without some way of wedging, or holding, the knife still she could not cut the ropes.

'Bring it over here,' said Lucien in a low voice.

Grasping the knife, she crawled over to Lucien.

'Hold it still,' he said.

'Ah!'

She saw what he intended. If she held the knife, then he could rub the ropes that bound his wrists over the blade.

She arranged herself with her back to him, so that she was kneeling behind him. The knife was at the right level to cut his ropes. Keeping it steady, she put just enough pressure on it to force it against his bonds. He moved his hands up and down, and the rope began to fray. At last it was cut through. He pulled his hands apart, and the rope fell away. Then she cut the rope that bound him to the chair back.

He turned and took the knife out of her hands, cutting the ropes around his ankles as well as those that bound him to the chair legs, and then gave his attention to Eleanor. She

234

could feel the warmth of his breath on her neck as he knelt behind her, cutting her bonds. At last they were done. Freeing her hands of the last vestiges of rope, she rubbed them together to restore her circulation.

'Are you all right?' he asked softly.

She nodded.

'Here. Let me see.'

He took her hands. With a frown he examined the red marks around her wrists. The rope had been tied tightly, and it had cut into her soft flesh. Kneeling beside her, with one knee raised, he exuded masculinity. His hair was as dark as a raven's wing and it was falling forward across his face. She could not see his expression. The moonlight filtering through the window was slight, and his face was shadowed. But when he lifted her hands her heart missed a beat. There could be no doubting his intention. He was going to place soft kisses on the red marks. His mouth hovered an inch from her wrist, and she tingled as she felt his breath. It was warm and caressing. And then he kissed her. His touch set her skin on fire. She should not respond to him but she could not help it.

His fingers closed round her own.

'I'm sorry I got you into this,' he said.

'If I remember rightly, I got myself into it.' Seeking to dispel the tension that hung in the air she added with a flash of humour, 'If I recall, it was my pig-headedness that was to blame!'

He smiled. 'Did I really call you pig-headed?'

'You did. And with good reason,' she admitted ruefully. 'You warned me about Mr Kendrick, but I refused to listen.'

'How could you, when you were protecting your sister?'

'Poor Arabella.' Eleanor's voice dropped. 'She will be dreadfully unhappy. I hope she does not believe what Mr Drayforth said. I would hate to think I have rescued her from one predicament, only to drag her into another.'

'Don't worry. She isn't alone. She is married now. Charles will help her.'

Eleanor was comforted.

A noise from the next room recalled them to the present.

Lucien dropped her hands and stood up. Striding over to the door, he put his eye to the rotten timbers. They were punctuated by holes. Some of the holes were small, made by woodworm. Others were large enough to look through.

A minute later he turned to her and said, 'There's only one ruffian in the next room.'

There came a rumbling sound from outside, accompanied by the clip clop of horses' hoofs.

'So that's it,' he said. 'Drayforth must have told the other two to move the carriage. He knows it will seem odd if it's seen outside one of the labourers' cottages. They must be taking it up to the main house.'

'And Drayforth?'

'My guess is that he has ridden back to his house. He probably wants to sleep and eat before returning to interrogate me. Once he starts, he won't be intending to stop until he's extracted everything he wants to know.'

Eleanor shuddered. The idea of Drayforth interrogating Lucien did not bear thinking about.

'Don't worry,' he said comfortingly. 'By the time he gets back we will no longer be here.'

His eyes warmed, and she felt herself smile. No matter how foolish it was, she could not help having feelings for him.

'If there is only one man guarding us, then now is the time for us to make our escape,' she said.

'It is. I'll go first. Wait here until I call you.'

She nodded.

He applied his eye to the hole in the door. Then, having ascertained exactly where their captor was, he took a step back from the door and with a flex of his powerful muscles he kicked it open, breaking the bar. The door flew back. Eleanor had a brief vision of the startled ruffian rising from his stool, and then Lucien wrestled him to the ground, knocking him out with one well-placed blow.

Rising, he turned to Eleanor and motioned her to stay still.

'It's possible only one of the others took the carriage back to the manor house,' he said in a low voice. 'We must be cautious. There might still be someone about.'

There was a window looking northward. Flattening himself against the wall, Lucien approached it carefully and looked out.

Eleanor held her breath. Would the other ruffian be there? And, if so, would he be dealt with as easily?

'I don't see anyone,' said Lucien.

He went over to the door. Opening it a crack, he looked out.

He turned to Eleanor. 'No one. Wait here, whilst I check it's safe outside.'

He was gone for a few minutes. Then he returned.

'It seems to be clear. There's a small wood not far from the cottage. We'll make for that. You will go first, and I will be right behind you. If by any chance the ruffians return, run straight for the trees and don't look back. Do you understand?'

Eleanor nodded. Although if Lucien needed help then nothing on earth would prevent her from turning back to give it to him.

'Good. Once under cover of the trees we can think about how to get back to Bath.'

They must do it as quickly as possible, Eleanor realized, and be seen going about their normal employments, before the rumour of their running away together had time to spread.

Lucien slipped out of the door. Eleanor followed. Together they looked round, checking again that there was no one there. Eleanor looked towards the small wood. It was no more than 200 yards away, and should be easy to reach. The ground in between was level, and whilst she would have to take care not to step on any of the abandoned gardening tools—a bent rake, a spade, and a broken hoe—and swerve a little to avoid a small tumbledown shed, the run should not prove too difficult.

Lucien motioned her to make a start.

Feeling secure in the knowledge that no one would be able to surprise her from behind, she lifted the hem of her gown and took to her heels. She had almost reached the shed, and was just congratulating herself on being half-way to the wood, when to her horror she saw one of the ruffians coming round the shed's corner.

He looked as startled as she was. And then he recovered himself and ran towards her with his arms outstretched. She swerved to avoid him and without stopping to look back, she ran on towards the trees. If she could just keep ahead of the ruffian, Lucien would deal with him.

Crack!

She felt a shock as a bullet whistled past her. The ruffian was firing at her. Then she heard another crack! and felt a sharp pain in her shoulder.

'Cur!' Lucien's voice was a snarl behind her.

There was the sound of a scuffle.

It began to grow fainter.

Oh, no, please, not now, she thought, as her head began to swim.

She clutched her shoulder, and looking down saw the hot red blood running through her fingers.

She fought to remain conscious, but it was no use. She felt herself beginning to sway.

And then a voice, strong and supportive, said, 'It's all right. I've got you.'

She was swept from her feet as Lucien scooped her up in his arms, his large body shielding her from further harm. He crossed the last yards of open ground and did not stop until they were hidden by the trees.

'I'm all right,' she said, as the trees closed around them.

'I'll be the judge of that.' His voice was full of concern.

He laid her gently down, setting her with her back against a tree. The pretty puffed sleeve of her ballgown was covered in blood.

'I'm going to have to examine the wound,' he said. His voice softened. 'It will mean cutting away your sleeve.'

She nodded.

'I will try not to hurt you, but I am afraid there will be some pain.'

'I understand.'

He produced his knife. With small, deft movements he cut the sleeve away from her arm, softly pulling back the fabric so that he could see how badly she was hurt. She bit her lip. The movement of the fabric over her torn flesh was proving painful. Then she saw the look of relief on his face and felt an answering sense of relief flow through her. It was clearly not as bad as he had feared.

'Thank God,' he said, 'it's just a flesh wound.'

He untied his cravat and pulled it off, forming it into a pad. Then he held it to her shoulder to halt the flow of blood.

There was such a look of tenderness on his face as he did it that she felt her heart flutter. But then, perhaps that was because she was injured, she told herself. He might be just as concerned for any other young lady who had been badly hurt.

'It needs something to hold it in place,' he said.

His eyes fell on the frill of her petticoat, which could be seen beneath the hem of her gown.

She gave a sigh. The petticoat was the only piece of pretty underwear she possessed. But still, it must be sacrificed.

'Go ahead,' she said.

With deft fingers he ripped the delicate fabric until he had a long strip in his hands.

Then expertly he wound it round the pad, binding it to her shoulder.

'You've done this before,' she remarked.

He gave a wry smile. 'Once or twice.' He tied the strip in a bow, then said, 'How do you feel?'

'I feel well.'

His smile became sincere, and his eyes warmed. 'You're a very courageous woman,' he said softly.

'I don't have much choice.' For some reason, his words made her feel vulnerable, and so she turned the compliment aside.

'Yes, you do. Young ladies always have a choice. They can have a fit of the vapours any time it suits them!'

He was teasing her, and she laughed. He stood up.

'I don't want to leave you,' he said, 'but I have to. I am going to fetch the horses.'

She looked surprised.

'There are two of them tied up behind the shed,' he explained. 'That's what the ruffian was doing. He was making sure they were securely tethered. Evidently two of the ruffians rode to the cottage. Which is lucky for us, because it means we can ride. Here. Take this.'

He handed her a pistol.

'I took it from one of the men. They should still be unconscious, but just in case one of them recovers and finds you here, I want you to have this. I don't expect you will have to use it, but if you must, then do it.'

Eleanor nodded. If either of the ruffians found her she would need to defend herself. Although it wasn't likely that they would do so, she reflected, looking round at the trees. She was inside the woodland, and well hidden by the fir trees.

He disappeared. Leaving her to face the fact that her feelings for him, instead of becoming less, were becoming increasingly complicated. To the physical attraction she had felt from the moment she had first set eyes on him was added a sense of complete trust; for although they were mixed up in a dangerous enterprise, she felt safe with her life in his hands.

She loosened the bow on her makeshift bandage a little, and saw to her relief that the blood flow had lessened but it had still not stopped. Pulling it tight once more—a difficult manoeuvre with only one hand, but one she managed—she waited for Lucien to return. He did not leave her alone for long. Before five minutes had passed he had returned with the two horses.

She tried to stand up, but feeling a little dizzy she was forced to sit down again.

'There's no hurry,' he told her. 'I used the rope that had bound us to tie up the ruffians. I had to knot it in several places where we had cut it, but there was still enough to do a thorough job.'

'I'm not sure I can ride,' she said.

'Then we'll ride together. I'll put you up in front of me and hold on to you.' His eyes looked into hers. 'I won't let you fall.'

'I know.'

Her words were simple, but provoked a tender glance. He seemed to be about to speak, but then the words died on his lips.

'Fortunately, I have a friend who lives nearby. We won't have to go more than four or five miles, and then you can rest.'

'No.' Eleanor shook her head. 'Arabella will be worried about me. I want to go back to Bath at once.'

'I'll get you home as soon as it's possible, but you can't go far with that wound. You're losing a lot of blood. You need to rest.'

'I can't be seen in this state,' she protested.

'Don't worry, my friend is discreet. He won't betray the fact that you were injured, or even that you visited his house. But he will give you somewhere safe to stay until you are well enough to travel onwards.'

'It hardly troubles me any more, and I am losing far less blood than I was,' she said stubbornly. She did not want to worry her sister, nor did she want to expose her to scandal. Or herself, either.

She stood up, determined to show him that she was all right, but she swayed on her feet, and almost fainted.

He caught her, and lifted her on to the

horse, mounting effortlessly behind her, before his strong arms slid round her waist.

'Lean back against me,' he said throatily.

'Your coat . . .' she protested.

'It's just a coat,' he said softly. 'Lean back, Eleanor.'

She gave a sigh and did as he said. It was a relief to be able to relax, and to let him take control. She had never been able to surrender herself to anyone before, but despite his recent coldness she felt she could surrender completely to Lucien. To her surprise, doing so made her feel stronger instead of weaker. It was as if she had relinquished something of great value, only to have it replaced with something of even greater worth.

He turned the horse and the animal set off at a gentle pace, picking its way through the narrow belt of woodland and at last emerging on the other side.

'Do you know where we are?' she asked.

He turned to look in every direction, taking care not to jolt her, then said, 'Yes. If we head north we will soon hit the road.'

'Is it safe to take the road?' she asked.

'It is now. We have skirted the point at which it joins with the drive of Drayforth's estate.'

'And if he goes to the cottage and discovers we have escaped?'

'Then he might find us on the road, it is true. But we would hear him coming, and we would be able to take cover in the trees on either side. It's our best route. I don't want to subject you to any more jolting than necessary, and the road is a much smoother surface to ride on than open countryside.'

The horse picked its way across country to the road. Lucien glanced both left and right, but there was nothing to be seen. Then he turned on to the road.

The going was easier, and Eleanor was grateful. Her shoulder was paining her and she was weak from loss of blood. But despite her pain, Eleanor enjoyed the beauty of the scene. The first stars could be seen in the sky. The tips of the trees sparkled where they caught the light.

At last they came to an imposing pair of stone gateposts to their right. Lucien turned the horse and they rode up the drive.

'Are you sure he won't mind you bringing me here?' she asked.

'We fought together on the Continent,' said Lucien simply.

'Ah.' Eleanor understood. The dangers the two men had shared had established a bond of trust between them, and they would always help each other if the need arose.

'And the servants?' she asked. Even if Lucien's friend would say nothing, she was uncertain whether the servants could be trusted.

'They have all been hand-picked for

trustworthiness; Will has been engaged in more than one dangerous enterprise of his own.'

She was content.

They rode up to the front of the house. It was a Palladian villa of elegant proportions made out of golden stone.

When the horse had come to a halt, Lucien dismounted carefully, supporting Eleanor with one hand whilst he did so. Then he lifted her down.

How strong he is, she thought, as he carried her. She would have liked to have walked into the house on her own two feet, but she felt very weak and knew she was not capable of it.

Lucien carried her up the steps.

At that moment the door was opened by an impassive butler, and a young man of about thirty years of age was revealed behind him.

'Lucien!' he exclaimed in astonishment. 'I saw you from the window. What the devil . . . ?'

His eyes went to Eleanor and then back again.

'No time to talk, Will,' said Lucien, striding into the house without more ado. 'She needs help.'

'Fetch Mrs Watkins at once,' said Will to the butler, rising to the occasion. 'And send one of the men for the doctor.'

The butler withdrew.

'In here,' said Will, leading the way into the drawing-room.

Lucien carried Eleanor into the room and laid her down on an elegant *chaise-longue.*

'What happened?' asked Will, once Eleanor was comfortably settled.

'It's a long story,' said Lucien.

'Then it can wait,' said Will, going over to the drinks' table and pouring out a glass of brandy. 'Here,' he said, kneeling next to Eleanor. 'Drink this.'

Eleanor pulled a face. She did not like strong spirits, but in the circumstances she knew she should drink the brandy.

She reached out her hand for the glass, but with her wounded shoulder the action made her wince.

Lucien took the tumbler from Will and held it gently to her lips.

She took a sip of the burning liquid and coughed. But then, as it started to revive her, she took another sip.

Watching the tender scene, Will looked at his friend in surprise. Then his face became thoughtful.

'I'll go and make sure the doctor's been sent for,' he said discreetly.

He went out of the room, leaving the two of them alone.

Eleanor finished the brandy and then lay back again.

'How do you feel?' he asked.

'Better,' she said.

He stroked her hair away from her face. In

all the turmoil her carefully arranged chignon had come loose, and her soft hair was falling about her shoulders.

'Eleanor . . .'

Something in his tone of voice made her turn her eyes to his.

'Yes?' Her voice was breathless.

'When I came to visit you . . .'

When he came to visit her? He had started to say something similar to her once before. What was it about his visit that preyed on his mind?

He pushed a stray strand of hair behind her ear.

'When I was on my way to see you, I saw . . .'

The door opened.

She felt Lucien's frustration. But on seeing that it was the housekeeper who had entered the room he stood up and strode over to the magnificent Adam fireplace, putting a discreet distance between them.

'The doctor has just arrived,' said the housekeeper. 'He will be in directly.'

The doctor came in a few minutes later. He was an elderly man with white hair and a kindly face. He was carrying a black bag.

As he crossed the room towards her, Eleanor was glad of the housekeeper's presence. It gave a respectability to the scene that would otherwise have been sadly lacking.

'Well, well,' said the doctor with a twinkle,

'what happened to you, miss? Got caught in the middle when the gentlemen were practising their shots, I hear.'

Eleanor realized that this was what Will must have told him in order to explain her injury.

'Gentlemen?' said the doctor.

Lucien hesitated and looked as though he wanted to stay, but Will took him by the arm and steered him towards the door. 'Of course, doctor,' Will said. 'We'll be in the library when you've finished.'

The two gentlemen left the room, whilst the housekeeper took a motherly seat by the side of the fireplace.

The doctor began his examination.

'Well, well, now, this has been bandaged quite well,' he said. 'Dear me, what a nasty thing to happen. You young ladies need to take more care when the gentlemen are shooting their pistols. You should really keep away from them. They are apt to show off to one another, and not notice what is going on around them.'

Having finished his examination, he said, 'Now, I am just going to clean it. It will hurt, I'm afraid, but you must be a brave girl. Never mind, it will soon be over.'

Eleanor gritted her teeth as the doctor cleaned her wound. Then he bandaged her shoulder once more.

'There, now we're done.' He turned to the

housekeeper. 'Would you ask the gentlemen to return? They will want to know how to look after the young lady until she has recovered.'

The housekeeper left the room, and returned a few moments later with Lucien and Will.

'How are you feeling?' asked Lucien, going over to Eleanor.

'Better,' she said.

'You look it. Your colour's starting to return.'

'Good. As soon as I can stand I must go home.'

'Eh? What's that?' asked the doctor with a frown. 'Go home?'

'The young lady is just visiting here, and is naturally anxious to be with her family at such a time,' interposed Will.

The doctor relented. 'I suppose so. But all the same, miss, you are in no condition to travel. How far do you have to go?'

'Not far,' she said. 'No further than Bath.'

He shook his head. 'You can't go yet. You must rest, and regain your strength.'

'But my sister will be worried about me,' she protested.

'She is expecting you back today, I gather?' he asked. 'Well, miss, if you can take a little supper and follow it with a glass of port, then as long as you rest you should be able to travel in an hour or two. But only in a private carriage, mind, and only if you are wrapped up well. You young ladies wear nothing but cobwebs these days,' he said paternally. He turned to Will. 'Make sure you tell your coachman to drive slowly, and avoid any pot-holes in the road.'

'I will.'

'And you, miss, must promise me to rest as soon as you get home.'

Eleanor readily gave her promise.

'Very well, then I see no harm in it.'

The housekeeper showed the doctor out.

'Are you sure you need to go home so soon?' asked Will solicitously. 'I could send one of my footmen with a message saying you have had an accident. You would be welcome to stay here until you have fully recovered. I have an aunt who lives nearby. She would be glad to come and stay for a few days, to protect your reputation.'

'Thank you, but I have to go.'

Will glanced at Lucien.

Lucien nodded. 'Unfortunately, it's necessary.'

'Then I'll get my cook to send you a little broth,' he said to Eleanor.

'Don't worry,' said Lucien, as Will followed the housekeeper out of the room. 'You will soon be with Arabella.'

But I will also be parted from you, she thought.

She tried to hide it from herself, but the thought of never seeing him again made her desolate.

She shivered.

'Here.' He took off his jacket and laid it over her.

The simple gesture, in its kindness and its gentleness, caused her even more pain. She was still unsure of him, not knowing what had caused his coldness at the wedding breakfast. Was it really that he had discovered he was raising expectations he had no intention of fulfilling? And was his subsequent behaviour nothing more than the behaviour of a man who is strongly attracted to a woman, but who cannot always restrain himself from touching her, even though he knows he should not do it? It could be so, but somehow she did not believe it. Although that could be self-delusion, a small voice whispered. She might be imagining that there was more to it than that, because she wanted there to be more.

His next words were no help in solving the conundrum.

'I know it hurts,' he said, 'but it will get better. Believe me.'

But what was he talking about? Was he talking about her damaged shoulder? Or, sensing what she felt for him, was he talking about her heart?

CHAPTER TEN

That night Will's carriage rolled slowly through the streets of Bath with its curtains drawn. Eleanor, lying comfortably inside, was wearing a cloak over her ballgown. It had been lent to her by Will, along with a travelling-rug, and they kept her warm. After eating a light supper and following it with a glass of port, she had been well enough to travel. And now here she was, almost back home.

Suddenly she felt apprehensive. What had happened whilst she had been away? Would Arabella and Charles have believed Drayforth's lies? And if they had, how would she be able to convince them otherwise without telling them the truth?

As the coach rattled along she wondered whether she should tell them just that. But it was not an idea she liked. Arabella would be worried, and feel guilty that she had been the unwitting cause of Eleanor's abduction, whilst Charles—no, she could not possibly explain to Charles. He knew nothing about the stolen letters, and therefore nothing about Mr Kendrick, so she could not tell him what had really happened without revealing Arabella's secret. And that was something she was determined not to do.

Then what should she say? What *could* she

say?

She decided at last that she must claim she had been ill and had gone home early, neglecting to tell anyone because she had been too poorly to think clearly. She did not like to lie, but some reason must be given for her sudden departure and it was the most convincing story she could think of. She would write a note to Arabella as soon as she got home to let her sister know that she was safe. And she would ask Arabella to call on her, so that she could set her sister's mind at rest.

The carriage rolled to a halt.

The footman Will had kindly sent with her opened the door and let down the step. Wrapping her cloak around her to hide her bandaged shoulder, Eleanor hurried into the house.

To her surprise, when she opened the front door she heard a cry of 'Eleanor!' and Arabella came flying out of the sitting-room.

'Eleanor! I have been so worried about you. I came home as soon as our guests had left, to find out if you were here. But what has happened? Where have you been? Come, let us go into the sitting-room. You look pale. Here, let me help you off with your cloak.'

'Careful,' began Eleanor. But it was too late. She winced as Arabella removed the cloak, dragging it across her bandaged shoulder.

Arabella gasped. 'What . . . ?' She looked at Eleanor in consternation.

'It's a long story,' said Eleanor.

'Oh, Eleanor. I never dreamt that you would have come to harm like this. But you are tired. You need to sit down.'

She arranged a chair with a footstool in front of it, and waited for Eleanor to sit down.

'And now, before you tell me what happened you must have some tea.' She went over to the bell.

Eleanor was surprised at Arabella's practical tone. It seemed that, in the last twenty-four hours, Arabella had started to grow up.

'Marriage must be good for you,' she said. 'You wouldn't have been able to take charge like that a few days ago.'

'I suppose I did not know what I could do until I tried,' Arabella replied.

'Does Charles know you are here?' asked Eleanor, hoping that her escapade had not put a strain on her sister's new marriage.

'Yes. Oh, Eleanor, I have told Charles everything. When you disappeared he was so understanding that I knew I could trust him completely, and I decided to tell him all about it.'

'About the letters?' asked Eleanor.

'About the letters, Mr Kendrick, everything,' said Arabella. 'I decided that if he was horrified with what I had to say and wanted an annulment then I would not oppose him, for if his love could not stand the truth then perhaps it wasn't the kind of love I really needed after all.'

'Goodness!' said Eleanor. It seemed that Arabella had grown up even more than she had guessed.

The door opened and Molly entered the room.

'Miss Grantham would like some tea,' said Arabella. Molly dropped a curtsy and left the room.

'Does she know I have been gone?' asked Eleanor.

'No. I thought it best not to tell her. No doubt she thinks you have just returned from the celebrations.'

'But tell me more about Charles,' said Eleanor. 'I take it he did not want an annulment,' she smiled.

'No.' Arabella laughed. 'He said he could not blame Thomas for falling in love with me, as he had done the same thing himself, and he could not blame me for having written such silly letters when I was young and foolish.' She smiled mischievously. 'And he said he would have to fulfil my craving for poetry by writing a sonnet to me himself.'

'Oh, Bella, I'm so pleased! I always felt it would be best if you could confide in Charles, but I was afraid that if he proved false it would break your heart.'

'And so it would have done,' Arabella said. 'But I am older now, and wiser.'

The door opened and Molly entered with a tray of tea.

Eleanor gratefully drank a cup of the refreshing beverage.

After she had finished it Arabella said, 'Now, tell me, Eleanor, what happened?'

'You did not believe Mr Drayforth's rumour, then, that I had run off with Lord Silverton?' asked Eleanor. 'I'm glad.'

Arabella flushed. 'I must confess that when you were nowhere to be found, and Lord Silverton had similarly disappeared, I wondered. But once I thought about it, of course I knew that you would never do such a thing. At least, not without telling me,' she said mischievously. She hesitated, then said, 'Was it something to do with Mr Kendrick?'

'Yes.'

'Charles thought it might have been. After I had told him everything he sent one of his most trusted servants to Mr Kendrick's Bath address and discovered that Mr Kendrick had been murdered a short time ago. Then he came here and questioned Cooper.'

'He knew that Cooper was here to protect us?'

'Not at first. But he suspected that Cooper was somehow involved, as he had appeared suddenly in our lives, and Cooper at last told Charles the truth.'

'Where is Cooper now?' asked Eleanor.

'With Charles, at Ormston House. They are

discussing what is best to be done. Oh, Eleanor, what a lot you didn't tell me.'

Eleanor sighed. 'I wanted to protect you. It wasn't a pleasant business, and I felt the less you knew the better. But perhaps now the time has come to tell you everything.'

Little by little Eleanor told her sister all about her adventures with Mr Kendrick, leading up to her recent abduction. The only thing she left out was that Lucien was working for the government and that Mr Kendrick, as well as being a blackmailer, had stolen military documents: that kind of information was best kept to herself.

'Well!' exclaimed Arabella, when she had finished. 'And to think, I never suspected Mr Drayforth. I thought he was a scandal-monger, but nothing else. I see now I was mistaken.' Her face fell. 'He won't come back, will he? You're not still in any danger?'

'No. Lu—Lord Silverton is taking care of him.'

Thoughts of Lucien made her grow quiet. He had handed her into the carriage with the utmost tenderness, but that had only made things harder as she did not know if she would ever see him again.

'Good.' Arabella heaved a sigh of relief. 'What an odious man he was. It was not enough for him to abduct you, he had to slander you as well, and all so that no one would think to look for you when they discovered you were missing.'

She took out her handkerchief, a pretty scrap of muslin, and twisted it in her hands.

Eleanor looked at her in surprise. She knew that gesture of old. It meant Arabella was worried.

'What is it?' she asked.

'Oh, nothing,' said Arabella nonchalantly. Then said in a rush, 'The thing is, Eleanor, it has created something of a scandal. In fact, the gossips are already calling it the Silverton scandal. There was a lot of talk this afternoon, and although Charles and I did everything we could to discourage it, still the rumour spread.'

'Then we must do what we can to dispel it,' said Eleanor practically.

Arabella nodded. 'I was thinking, if you are well enough, we ought to take a turn in the carriage tomorrow. If people see you taking the air as though nothing has happened, they will believe that nothing has happened. I will go back to Ormston House now and tell Charles and Cooper that you have returned, but I will call again tomorrow and I will bring Charles with me. We will need his countenance if we are to silence the scandalmongers.'

'I'm sorry to bring this on you, particularly on your wedding day,' said Eleanor.

'Pish!' said Arabella.

'All that matters is that you are safe.'

She stood up.

'Rest now,' she said. 'Charles and I will call

for you tomorrow.'

*   *   *

Shortly after handing Eleanor into the carriage, Lucien took his leave of Will and set off to deal with Drayforth.

His mind was in turmoil. What had he really seen in the gardens? he asked himself for the hundredth time. He had seen Eleanor embracing a strange young man, and from that he had deduced that she was in love with him. But everything he had seen since pointed against it. So much so that he had been determined to ask her about what he had seen.

He had tried to speak to her about it on several occasions, but the circumstances had never been favourable. First of all they had been abducted, and then they had been tied up, or running for their lives. And after that, Eleanor had been injured. He had almost asked her when handing her into the carriage, but then he had controlled himself, knowing he must give her time to recover from her ordeal. How long must he give her? That was the question that plagued him. Until she was fully recovered? No, he knew he would not be able to wait that long. He had to know soon, because until he did, he would have no peace of mind. Did she love the man she had been embracing? Or did she—could she ever—love *him*?

Dressed in her best carriage-dress, Eleanor sat by Arabella and Charles as they took the air the following afternoon. As the carriage turned down a fashionable thoroughfare, Eleanor's appearance caused a stir. There were whispers and glances, but no one stopped to speak to the party and one or two people actually turned their horses' heads away. After a few minutes of this, Charles decided to take a hand. Thumping on the floor of the carriage with his cane, he signalled it to stop next to Lady Chawford.

'Good afternoon, Lady Chawford,' he said pleasantly. 'It's a fine day we're having.'

Lady Chawford, taking a walk with her companion, stood as still as a statue. But then, evidently deciding that the goodwill of a future duke should not be lost, she inclined her head and remarked that it was a very fine day indeed.

Charles repeated the manoeuvre with a number of other notable people, and although their replies were cool they spoke to him. He made it unavoidable that they spoke to Eleanor, too. But Eleanor knew that if she had been on her own they would have cut her.

It was a lowering thought.

'Well, we've done what we can,' said Charles, as at last the carriage turned back to

Eleanor's home. 'We must just hope it is enough to scotch the rumours. I had hoped that Silverton might have paid a call. He could save your reputation instantly if he had a mind to . . . but no matter.'

Eleanor said nothing. The thought of Lucien saving her reputation filled her with dread, for there was only one way he could do it: by offering her his hand. To have him offer it to her for the right reasons would have filled her with happiness. But to have him offer it for the sake of her reputation—it didn't bear thinking about.

The carriage came to a halt outside the Granthams' house and the three of them went inside.

They had just divested themselves of their coats when there came the sound of a carriage rolling to a halt outside.

'Oh, no. Not someone come to crow over us in our misfortune,' said Arabella anxiously.

Charles went over to the window.

'No,' he said. 'It's the one person I had hoped to see. The one man who can put an end to this mess and save Eleanor's reputation. It's Lord Silverton.'

'He has come to offer you his hand,' said Arabella to Eleanor.

Charles nodded. 'As a gentleman, he can do no less.'

'No.' Eleanor spoke out loud. Her revulsion to the idea was so strong that the word came out bluntly.

'No?' enquired Charles. It was clear he had misunderstood her. 'Then you can think of another way for him to save your reputation?'

Eleanor regained control of herself with difficulty. 'That is not what I meant.' She took a deep breath. 'I meant that I cannot marry him.'

'Of course you can.' Charles spoke kindly. 'I know it's not ideal Eleanor—no one wants to be coerced into marriage—but like it or not, your reputation has been tarnished, and Silverton must take steps to protect it.'

'No.' Eleanor's voice was as heavy as lead.

'Come now, it won't be as bad as all that. I know Silverton has a wild reputation, but he's an honourable man, and you will have nothing to complain of as his wife. I was at school with him, and I know him to be sound. He will not ill-treat you. On the contrary, I suspect he will treat you very well. He is rich and titled. As his wife you will have a position in Society, and a house in town. It will be all right, you'll see.'

'You don't understand,' cried Eleanor, realizing that Charles had misunderstood the reasons for her reluctance to marry Lucien.

'Ah. You think he will resent you because he has been forced to marry you. But I don't think that will be the case. He needs to settle down sometime: his nurseries need filling, and that cannot happen until he takes a wife. You are a respectable young lady with good connections. He can have no objection to the match. In fact, if I may say so, I think he will do far better in marrying you than he would have done if he had had a free choice.' Charles smiled kindly. 'Ten to one he would have chosen someone wildly unsuitable and would have been miserable for the rest of his days!'

Eleanor's spirits plummeted. This was even worse. But there was nothing she could do about it. She could not tell Charles what was really worrying her, and so she must try and put a good face on it.

Besides, there was not time for anything more, as Lucien was already being announced.

'We will leave you for a short while,' said Charles discreetly. He took Arabella's arm. 'If you need assistance, you have only to pull the bell.'

Eleanor nodded miserably.

Arabella looked at her sister with concern, but then accompanied Charles out of the room.

A minute later Lucien strode in. His clothes were crumpled, and there was an air of urgency about him that made her heart turn over. His face, shaped by its high cheekbones and dimpled chin, was etched with an emotion that made him look more vibrantly alive than she had ever seen him. But what that emotion was she could not decide.

'Eleanor.' He stood looking at her, then said, 'Forgive me. I had to come.'

Her spirits sank. 'I know.' As Charles had said, hearing of the scandal, he had had no alternative but to come and see her and offer her the protection of his name.

'Then you have been expecting me.'

She nodded. To postpone the evil moment, she said, 'Will you take some tea.'

'Tea?' He looked surprised.

'I can ring for some refreshment if you would like some,' she persevered.

'No. I haven't come here for tea.'

He was about to continue when she forestalled him by saying, 'Won't you take a seat?'

He hesitated, then sat down on a Hepplewhite chair. His long legs were stretched in front of him, and his breeches were pulled tightly across them. His boots were spattered with mud.

The sight gave her inspiration.

'Tell me, have you succeeded in catching Drayforth?' she asked, as she, too, perched on the edge of a chair.

He looked perplexed, as though this was not what he had come to talk about, but he could not avoid replying to her question. 'Yes. Will sent a messenger to bring reinforcements, and I led them to Drayforth's house. He was just about to set out to interrogate me.'

'It must have come as a terrible shock to him.'

'It did.' Lucien's voice was grim. 'He

266

thought he had taken care of everything.'

His face darkened, and she could tell he was replaying the scene.

'He put up a determined fight. He had a number of ruffians in the house, and for a while it looked as though he might escape, but a stray bullet caught him in the leg, and then we had him.'

'And the general?' Eleanor asked.

'It wasn't easy to get Drayforth to divulge his whereabouts. He tried to use the general's life to bargain for his own. But in the end we didn't need him to tell us. We searched all his addresses, and found the general in the attic of Drayforth's town house.'

'Was he hurt?'

'He had not been treated well. But he wasn't badly injured, and he will make a full recovery.'

Eleanor nodded. 'Good.'

Lucien started to speak, and to forestall him she said, 'And the two men we saw at Mr Kendrick's house?'

'They were simply there to reclaim some letters. Kendrick had been blackmailing their sister, and they had gone to his house in order to demand their return. On finding the house was empty, they took the letters and left without ever knowing that Mr Kendrick was dead.'

'Then everything has turned out for the best,' said Eleanor.

'Yes.'

There was an uncomfortable silence.

Then he broke out, 'Eleanor, I have not come here to talk to you about Drayforth. I have come here to ask you to marry me.'

It was the moment she had been waiting for, and the one she had been dreading. In order to protect her reputation he was offering to make her his wife. But she could not go through with it. She could not accept his hand, and read the notice of their betrothal in *The Times*. She could not make arrangements for the wedding, stand next to him in a church, live in his home, bear his children, knowing all the while that he did not love her.

So she gathered all her strength, and said, 'I can't.'

Beneath his olive complexion he went white. 'You can't?'

She swallowed. 'No.'

She looked at him across the distance of a few feet, and it felt as though it was a hundred miles.

'So you're to marry him.'

His voice came out as a groan.

She was puzzled. What did he mean?

'I don't understand,' she said.

'I saw you together. In Sidney Gardens,' he explained. 'I had hoped . . . but no matter. Now I understand.'

Sidney Gardens? She cast her mind back. She had not been in Sidney Gardens since she had met Thomas. She remembered Thomas's exuberant embrace. So Lucien had seen that? Yes, he could have done. He had been on his way to her house, to visit her, and he would have had to pass close by the gardens. It would explain a great deal.

She was about to tell him the truth of the matter when she realized that here was a way out of her terrible predicament. By going along with his suggestion that she was to marry Thomas she would have a reason for refusing Lucien's hand, and then she would not have to endure the exquisite torture of becoming his wife. For that's what it would be, to marry him without his love. A kind of torture.

'Are you sure he will stand by you?' Lucien said in a low voice. 'After such a scandal, are you sure he will not abandon you? Because I will not.'

The huskiness of his voice set her insides quivering. But she must not give in to it. She must be strong.

'Quite sure. We have known each other since my family moved to Bath. Thomas's family was one of the first to make us welcome, and we have been friends ever since. He will not let me down.'

She hoped that Lucien would now leave. But he did no such thing. Instead his eyes looked directly into her own. 'And do you love him?' he asked.

She could not answer him. So she turned

away from him, and walked over to the fireplace. But he followed her. He placed his hands gently on her shoulders and turned her round.

'Do you love him?' he asked again.

She knew she must say yes. End it. But with his eyes looking so deeply into her own she could not lie to him. And yet she must say something.

Pulling away from him, she gave a light laugh.

'Love? What is love?' she asked. 'Something for poets to make verses about.'

She hoped she was fooling him. She was certainly not fooling herself.

'Are you so certain that is all it is?' he asked.

It would be so much easier if only he was not standing so close to her. She could feel the nearness of him, even though he was no longer touching her. She could feel the heat of him. She longed to go to him. And the longing was becoming more and more difficult to contain.

This was dangerous. She must bring the conversation to a speedy end. And to do so she must finally find the strength to lie.

'Yes,' she replied. 'I am twenty-six years old. If it was real then I would have found it by now.'

'And haven't you?'

The question was a direct challenge.

Her eyes flew to his, and for one insane moment she wanted to answer him honestly.

She wanted to say, *Yes. I have. I've found it with you.* But she could not do it. She must maintain the charade, so that he would accept that she would not marry him. So summoning all her courage, she said, 'No.'

An unfathomable look crossed his face.

She wanted to go to him. Touch him. But she must not. She must stand there like a statue; aloof, reserved, cold.

At last he recovered his composure.

'Then there is no more to be said.'

He gave her one last glance, full of an emotion she could not read, let alone begin to understand, and then strode out of the room.

Eleanor remained standing for one more minute and then collapsed on to the sofa. She had done it. She had rejected him. But it had cost her every last ounce of her strength.

*   *   *

'You refused him?' Arabella was aghast.

She had come back into the room once Lucien had left, and was looking at Eleanor in concern.

'Yes.'

'Oh, Eleanor, do you think you were wise? I know it is not what you had once hoped for from marriage, but you were not made to be single. And Lord Silverton is an honourable man. I know you do not love him, but . . .' and then she broke off. 'Oh!' Her eyes opened wide. There was a dawning of understanding. 'So that's it. You do love him. Now I understand.'

Eleanor nodded. 'So you see, Bella, there can be no question of my marrying him, knowing that he does not love me.'

'No. I see that. It would be too dreadful.' Her face was stricken. But then her tone became determinedly cheerful. 'Never mind, there will be someone else for you, you'll see. Charles and I will have lots of balls and parties when we return from the Lake District and you will come to them all. And don't forget we have a house in London. You will stay with us for the Season. There are a lot of nice young gentlemen in London,' she said encouragingly. 'You will soon forget all about Lord Silverton and fall in love with someone else.'

'Of course.' Eleanor spoke bracingly.

But she knew, and Arabella knew, that she lied.

*　　　*　　　*

Lucien felt numb as he left Ormston House. He had hoped against hope that Eleanor loved him, and that she would accept his hand in marriage, but all such hopes had been dashed.

He had not meant to visit her so soon. He had meant to wait a few days, so that she would have had time to rest and recover her strength. But he had not been able to wait. He

272

was in love with her, and he had not been able to bear the suspense of waiting to discover whether or not she was in love with him. And so he had gone to visit her, and learnt the worst. That she was not in love with him. That she was going to marry Thomas.

He ground his teeth. How could she marry that dandified fop?

But what did it matter *how* she could do it? She could. And that one fact had destroyed his happiness and peace of mind. All he could do now was bury himself in his work. Tie up the loose ends of the Drayforth affair; weed out Drayforth's associates; and embark on some new mission which would distract his thoughts from his unbearable pain.

CHAPTER ELEVEN

Eleanor wandered over to the window. Cooper could be seen outside, digging over the garden. Until all of Drayforth's associates had been rounded up there was a possibility she was in danger, and he had instructions to remain.

His presence reminded her of Lucien. She turned away from the window. The handsome lord was someone she would rather forget. She gave a hollow laugh. Forget him? That was impossible. But still she must do her best to put him out of her mind.

She turned her thoughts away from such a painful subject and fixed them firmly on the garden. As she was to have Cooper with her for some time longer, she decided she would ask him to create some extra flower beds. If she reorganized the garden it would give her something to occupy her mind.

*   *   *

Lucien remained in London throughout the months of October and November. Tidying up the loose ends surrounding Drayforth's capture mercifully kept him occupied and left him little time to dwell on Eleanor's rejection of his hand. Which was just as well, as it had caused him ferocious despair. He had never known love before, and he had certainly not been looking for it, but when he had met Eleanor he had discovered feelings he had never known he possessed. She had aroused in him a sense of admiration as she had dealt with one dangerous situation after another, overcoming them with boundless courage. She had stirred his passions. And she had aroused in him a hitherto unknown instinct that had made him fiercely protective; a desire to make her his mate. She made him want to wed her and bed her; to hold her close and never let her go.

But she had refused him.

He must not dwell on it. He must turn his

274

thoughts aside. But he could not do it. It preyed on his mind. She wasn't in love with Thomas. She had admitted it. And yet she was going to marry him anyway. They had known each other since she had moved to Bath, and they had been friends for years, she had said. Damn it all, didn't she know that wasn't enough?

The insane desire to go to Bath and convince her that she couldn't marry such a fop came over him, as it had done every day since their last meeting, and it was only with the greatest difficulty that he managed to fight it down. Again and again he thought over her words.

Love, she had said. What is love?

It was strange. For a time he had been convinced that she *had* been in love, and in love with him, but yet she had declared that she had never known that emotion. Could it really have been nothing more than arrogance that had led him to think it? It must have been. And yet he still found that difficult to believe. He was not usually deceived about women's feelings. But then, Eleanor was like no other woman he had ever known.

The door opened and Beddows walked in. 'The carriage is here, my lord,' he said.

Lucien withdrew his thoughts from their dark channels with difficulty. 'Thank you, Beddows.'

Forcing his face into a normal expression,

275

he put on his caped greatcoat and went out to his carriage, then headed off for his club. He was due to meet the general, and to discover whether the last of Drayforth's associates had been captured, thus putting an end to the matter once and for all.

As he climbed out of his carriage, however, he was shocked to see Thomas on the pavement, just about to head into the same club. Only the greatest effort prevented a snarl from appearing on his face. But he must be polite. This was Eleanor's intended, and no matter how bereft he was at the knowledge that she was to marry this ridiculous fop, he would not wound her by cutting her fiancé.

'Hello, Silverton,' said the younger man politely. Then, seeing that Lucien did not know his surname, he continued, 'Darby. We met at Arabella's wedding.'

'Darby.' Lucien tried to make it sound as though the meeting was a pleasure and not a torment.

Thomas proffered his hand and Lucien took it, resisting the urge to crush the younger man's hand in his vicelike grip.

'I want to thank you for helping Eleanor to retrieve those dreadful letters,' said Thomas.

'Think nothing of it.'

Lucien's manner, whilst polite, was not welcoming, but Thomas did not seem to notice. He fell into step beside Lucien as the two of them went into White's.

Lucien was torn between a desire to get away from Thomas as quickly as possible, before he said or did something unforgivable, and a desire to ask about Eleanor and find out how she was. He had not seen her since the day of his disastrous proposal and he wanted to make sure that she had recovered from her wound. He wrestled with himself for a moment, telling himself that it was better not to know, and to put her out of his mind. But in the end he could not resist. 'How is she? he asked.

Thomas sighed. 'As beautiful as ever,' he said.

Lucien clenched his fists but said nothing.

'I don't mind telling you, Silverton, I think she's an angel. Her eyes—heavenly! And her smile—enchanting! Marriage suits her.'

'Marriage?' Lucien went white. Oh, God, the deed was done. She was married. And Thomas, this undeserving fop, was her husband! He fought down an urge to knock the man down. He should leave, get away. But he could not do it. Painful as it was, he had to know more. 'When was the wedding?' he asked, in what he hoped was a normal voice.

Darby looked at him strangely. 'Why, last month, of course.'

'In October?' Ah! It was too terrible. So she had married Thomas almost as soon as she had rejected him. It had given her no pause for thought, then, his proposal. It had not made her reconsider, or delay. Then she could never have had any feelings for him after all. The knowledge was devastating.

'Of course,' said Thomas, looking at him more strangely than ever. 'Don't you remember?'

'Remember?' asked Lucien, wondering if Thomas thought he had been invited. That would have been the final straw, if he had actually been expected to attend.

'Are you foxed?' asked Thomas. 'You must remember. You were there.'

'There?' asked Lucien, astonished.

'Of course. In the abbey.'

Lucien started to breathe again, and his colour began to return. 'You were talking about *Arabella*?'

'Yes. She's a beauty. I wrote an ode to her hair, and a sonnet to her eyes! Charles is a lucky man.'

'Quite so,' Lucien agreed mechanically. Against all reason, his hopes were beginning to rise. 'But I was not talking about Arabella. I was talking about Miss Grantham. Miss *Eleanor* Grantham,' he said, to make sure there could be no further mistake. 'I have not seen her for quite some time. I was wondering whether she was well.'

'Oh, Eleanor!' said Thomas. 'I see! We were at cross purposes. Yes, she's well. In fact, she's very well. Or at least, I suppose she is.'

His words startled Lucien. 'You suppose?'

'Well, I can't say for certain. I haven't seen her since the day of the wedding.'

'Not seen her since the *wedding*?'

'No.' Thomas looked at him curiously. 'Are you *sure* you're not foxed?'

'Perfectly. It's just that I'm surprised you have not seen Miss Grantham.' He wrestled with himself, and then ground out through clenched teeth, 'I thought you and she were engaged.'

Thomas's eyebrows shot up in astonishment. 'Eleanor and I engaged? What on earth gave you that idea?'

'I . . . don't know.'

'No, I can never marry, alas! I am wedded to my art.'

'Then you are not betrothed to Miss Grantham?' asked Lucien, trying vainly to suppress a smile.

'No. Nor ever have been. You must have heard talk of Arabella's betrothal and somehow got confused,' said Thomas, with the air of one who has just solved a thorny problem to his satisfaction.

'Very probably,' said Lucien, no longer able to suppress his smile and letting it break out all over his face.

So Eleanor was not betrothed to Thomas. What's more she never had been. Then why . . . ?

He did not know. But nothing on earth was going to stop him finding out.

Eleanor was in her garden in Bath, supervising Cooper as he created a new flower-bed. Thankfully his services had not been needed in a protective capacity, but Eleanor reflected that the house and garden had never been in such a wonderful state. Unfortunately, the same could not be said of her emotions.

She had tried to put all thoughts of Lucien out of her mind, but she had failed. He was like no other man she had ever met. He filled her with the strongest and most wonderful feelings she had ever known. She had endured some very dangerous and difficult circumstances since meeting him, but she would not have changed a minute of their time together. Everything about him made her want him more. She loved him. She trusted him. She desired him. She wanted to spend every day of her life with him. And yet she had to resign herself to the fact that she would never see him again.

Should she have accepted his hand? That was the question that plagued her, as it had plagued her every waking minute since she had turned him down. True, it would have been painful for her, to marry him knowing he did not love her. But was this any better? Never seeing him, never touching him . . . never even hearing of him?

She recalled her thoughts from their useless wanderings. What was done was done. She could not change the past. She turned her attention with difficulty back to the garden plan she held in her hand. With some new flower-beds, some choice new plants, and a judicious rearrangement of the ones she had, she would be able to make it truly lovely. It would help to ease her spirit in the difficult months to come. Or so she hoped.

She wandered down to the gate, where she was planning to plant a bed of scented flowers. She was just deciding whether to have them on both sides of the gate, or only on one, when she was distracted by the sound of a horse coming up the lane. It was unusual enough to make her lift her head, for the only horses that passed as a general rule were those belonging to the doctor or the rector, if they had to make a call. She was just wondering which one of these two worthy gentlemen it would be when the horse rounded the corner.

Lucien!

Against all reason her spirits soared. His black hair, falling in a lock across his forehead, was wild and untamed. His body, long and lean, exuded masculine strength. Her heart began to race.

He had not yet seen her. But at any moment he would do so.

She hurriedly swept her cap from her head, pushing a stray tendril of hair back behind her ears and patting the small curls that softened her forehead into place.

And then he turned his head.

She longed to run towards him, to be swept up into his arms and placed in front of him on his horse. She still remembered how it felt to be held in his embrace, and the memory was wonderful. But then she told herself to be sensible. All such times had passed. He must have come to take Cooper.

The thought, likely though it was, deflated her. She had hoped for one impossible moment that he had come to see her. But common sense told her that he had tied up the last lingering threads of the Drayforth affair, and had come to tell Cooper that he was no longer needed in Bath.

Schooling her face into a polite expression, instead of the joyful expression it had worn on first seeing him, she prepared to greet him. She would be cool, calm and collected. She would let him know nothing of the turbulent emotions that were swirling in her breast. She would not make him feel obliged to repeat his offer and press her to take his hand in marriage. For if he did, she knew she would not be strong enough to resist.

She stilled her fluttering heart as he drew level with the gate. He dismounted, then tethered his horse to a nearby tree.

'Luc—' she began, before remembering herself. 'Lord Silverton,' she said formally.

They were separated by the gate, but even so she could not prevent her wayward thoughts from imagining him leaning over it, taking her face in his hands and kissing her deeply . . .

She gathered herself together. 'This is a pleasant surprise.'

His eyes roved over her face, drinking in every line and every curve. They roamed over her brow, following its breadth and clarity before dropping to her nose, and then caressing her flushed cheeks. They lingered there for a moment and then fell still further, to her lips.

Why did he have to make her feel like this? she thought, as her heart began to pound in her chest. Was it not bad enough that she must love him unrequited, his mind, his spirit and his soul? Did she really have to react so strongly to his body as well? It generated an aura so powerful that it robbed her of rational thought. She could not think. She could not breathe. She could only imagine him taking her in his arms and kissing her.

His eyes came to rest on hers.

Her heart missed a beat. There was such an openness about them that without understanding why, she was afraid.

'Is it?' he asked in a husky voice.

She swallowed. She must speak. But her lips were dry.

'Of course,' she managed to say at last.

There was something in the way he was

looking at her that made her aware he found her answer significant.

Flustered, she sought refuge in the commonplace. 'Won't you come in?'

His gaze held hers for a moment more. Then he said, 'Thank you.'

She opened the gate and began to walk towards the house, leaving him to fall into step. She had hoped that she would feel better when they were going back to the house, but instead she felt worse. He moved with the predatory grace of a jungle cat and she could feel the power of him as he strode along beside her.

She would feel safer when she was inside, she told herself. She could bid him be seated, and then she could sit as far away from him as possible—on the other side of the room.

'You have come to take Cooper away, I suppose,' she said, as she led him into the sitting-room.

He did not reply.

She should speak again, ask him to sit down, but it was impossible. She could do nothing but stand there, daring neither to move nor speak. Because if she did, she was afraid she would do or say something she would regret.

And then he took her gently by the shoulders and turned her to face him. 'It isn't Cooper I've come to talk to you about.'

Her eyes fell to the floor. She could not meet his gaze, because if she saw his eyes there would be no room for anything but complete honesty between them. And complete honesty was something she dreaded.

He reached out one strong finger and lifted her chin. He said, 'I came to talk about you.'

She felt her legs grow weak. She tried to speak but no words came out. She tried again. 'Me?' she asked.

'Yes.' His voice was low. 'You.'

He took his finger away from her chin and brushed it across the line of her cheek. 'And me.' His finger trailed across her lips. 'And us.'

It felt so wonderful that she longed to take his hand and kiss it. But she must not do it. Not until she understood him. Because once she gave herself to him there would be no turning back. She would surrender herself completely.

'Us?' she asked. Her voice was no more than a whisper.

'Yes, Eleanor,' he said softly. 'Us.'

'I don't know what you mean.'

'I think you do.' An unfathomable spark lit his eyes and he said in a different tone of voice, 'I see you have not yet married Thomas.'

'Ah.' She felt a guilty flush spring to her cheek.

'Tell me, Eleanor, why did you say you were going to marry him?'

'Oh, that was . . .' She tried to sound airy and dismissive, but instead, her voice caught in her throat.

'That was?' he asked.

'That was a . . . misunderstanding,' she prevaricated.

'No. It was a lie. What I want to know,' he said caressingly, 'is why?'

She could not bring herself to meet his gaze, but when he lifted her chin she had no choice. She had to look into his eyes. She had to be honest. All her defences were stripped away. She summoned her courage and said, 'Because I couldn't bear it—the thought of marrying you.'

There was silence, and the air was tense.

'You couldn't bear the thought of marrying me?' His steely blue eyes searched her own.

She swallowed. 'No.'

'Why not?'

His voice was throaty, and her knees went weak.

'Because . . .' she said.

'Yes?'

He was standing so close now that she had to tilt her head back to look up at him. His long, powerful body, was pressed distractingly against hers.

'Because it would not have been right.'

'And why is that?'

'Because of your reason for asking me.'

He lifted his hand and pushed back a curl of hair. 'You don't know what my reason was,' he said.

286

It was difficult to think with him standing so close to her, let alone to speak. But she must do it. 'You are wrong. I do. You wanted to protect me from the scandal.'

'The scandal?'

'Yes.' She persevered, though her heart was hammering in her chest and her senses were swimming with the nearness of him. 'You heard the rumours. They spread rapidly after Drayforth said we had run off together.'

'And you think that's why I asked you to marry me?'

'I do.'

'And you think that was the wrong reason for asking you to marry me?' he enquired as his hand cupped the back of her head and his strong fingers tangled themselves in her hair.

His touch made her shiver from head to foot. Nevertheless she looked him in the eye, 'Yes.'

'Then tell me,' he said, 'what is the right reason?'

He was looking at her with an almost unbearable intensity.

'The right reason . . .'

He waited, all brooding male, whilst she gathered herself.

'The right reason,' she went on resolutely, stepping back so that he could not touch her, though her body cried out for him to do so. 'Though I dare say you will think it ridiculous—the right reason is for love.'

'And why should I find that ridiculous?'

'Because you don't love me.'

'Oh, yes, I do. I asked you to marry me for one reason and one reason only. Because I do love you.'

Her eyes lit with an overwhelming joy.

He pulled her into his arms. 'I have loved you since the moment I met you. Everything that happened before that had been meaningless; a shadow play. But this is real.'

His lips met her own and she was lost. His kiss pulled her deeper, dragging her under to a world of new and wonderful sensations that she found herself longing to explore.

At last he let her go.

'I, too, think there is only one reason for marriage,' he said. 'I have told you that I love you. The question now remains, do you love me?'

'Oh, yes, Lucien,' she sighed, as she returned his passionate kiss. 'I do.'

When at last they parted, he sat down by the fireplace and pulled her on to the sofa next to him.

Eleanor gave a sigh of contentment and rested her head on his shoulder.

'If only I had known that you loved me, I would have accepted your hand straight away,' she said. 'Why didn't you tell me?'

'How could I, when you laughed at the very idea of love?'

'That was not well done of me. But when

you asked me if I was in love with Thomas, I couldn't bring myself to lie to you by saying that I was. So I had to pretend love was unimportant, that it did not even exist.'

'Then tell me something, if you were not in love with Thomas, why were you embracing him in Sidney Gardens?'

'Are you jealous?' she teased him.

'Now that I know you are in love with me,' he said, giving her a hug . . . which led to a kiss . . . and then another kiss . . . 'I am not jealous of anyone.'

'Thomas has an artistic temperament,' she said, nestling into his arms. 'He has been writing poetry since he was a little boy. He wanted to thank me for retrieving the compromising letters Arabella had written to him, and when he did so he did it in his usual effusive way, throwing his arms around me and holding me tight. I responded in kind: we have known each other for years, and it was like hugging a brother.'

'A brother?' Lucien enquired, one eyebrow raised.

'Yes.'

'Ah, good. Then I can meet him again without being tempted to knock him down!'

'You weren't!' exclaimed Eleanor in mock horror.

'I was.'

'Poor Thomas!'

Lucien laughed. 'Poor Thomas is quite safe

from me. In fact, I owe him a debt of gratitude.'

'You do?'

He nodded. 'It was because of Thomas I came to see you. I met him outside my club. I could not avoid speaking to him, and at last I gave into the overwhelming temptation to ask how you were.'

'And he was astonished?'

'Yes.'

'And denied that we were betrothed?'

'Yes.' His voice was softer this time.

Eleanor's own voice softened in response.

'And so you came to see me.'

'To see you, and to make you mine.'

His voice was by now so soft she could barely hear it, but the whisper of his breath on her skin set her senses on fire.

'Name the day for the wedding,' he said.

'We will have to wait for Arabella and Charles to return from the Lake District.' She smiled mischievously. 'Arabella made me promise I would not get married until she came home!'

'She knew about us?'

'She guessed.'

'Very well, then we will wait for her to return. But not a moment longer.'

Eleanor agreed, then gave herself up to his kiss.

We hope you have enjoyed this Large Print book. Other Chivers Press or Thorndike Press Large Print books are available at your library or directly from the publishers.

For more information about current and forthcoming titles, please call or write, without obligation, to:

Chivers Large Print
published by BBC Audiobooks Ltd
St James House, The Square
Lower Bristol Road
Bath BA2 3SB
UK
email: bbcaudiobooks@bbc.co.uk
www.bbcaudiobooks.co.uk

OR

Thorndike Press
295 Kennedy Memorial Drive
Waterville
Maine 04901
USA
www.gale.com/thorndike
www.gale.com/wheeler

All our Large Print titles are designed for easy reading, and all our books are made to last.